Audrey's Big Secret

The Audrey Club!

If you love reading *Audrey* stories, join Audrey's fan club to read more!

- You will receive a postcard from Audrey!
- FREE updates on Audrey via *The Outback Post*.
- Enter Audrey competitions.
- FREE Audrey giveaways.
- The chance to have the author, Christine Harris, visit your school.

To join send your mailing address inside an envelope to:
Little Hare Books, 8/21 Mary Street,
Surry Hills, NSW, 2010
or email Audrey on: audrey@audreyoftheoutback.com.au

*You will need to get Mum or Dad or your guardian to send a permission note in your email or envelope!

I love your books. I can't get my eyes away from them!—Greta Owen, age 9

Audrey's Big Secret

Christine Harris

Illustrations by Ann James

LITTLE HARE
www.littleharebooks.com

To my parents, Glenn and Bunty, who showed me that
we are all brothers and sisters in one big family—CH

For Mandy Cooper—AJ

Little Hare Books
8/21 Mary Street, Surry Hills
NSW 2010 AUSTRALIA

www.littleharebooks.com

Text copyright © Christine Harris 2009
Illustrations copyright © Ann James 2009
Cover illustration copyright © Ann James 2009

First published in 2009

National Library of Australia
Cataloguing-in-Publication entry

Harris, Christine, 1955- .

Audrey's big secret / Christine Harris ; illustrator, Ann James.

978 1 921272 53 0 (pbk.)

For primary school age.

Country life—South Australia—Juvenile fiction.
Stolen generations (Australia)—Juvenile fiction.

James, Ann.

A823.3

Cover design by Natalie Winter
Set in 13/18pt Stone Informal by Clinton Ellicott
Printed in Australia by Griffin Press, Adelaide

5 4 3 2 1

Molly Kr Grealy.

About the Author

Christine Harris has lived in different parts of South Australia, some of them isolated country areas.

The directions to one of her houses went like this: 'the first fridge on the right, fifteen kilometres after the last pub'. Kangaroos jumped past her kitchen window, and she once found a snake skin in the shed.

She spent much of her childhood in the wild places of her imagination, as a princess in a castle, a pirate on the wild seas, an archaeologist. Even her best friend, Jennifer Hobbar, was imaginary. But Christine only realised this when she tried to visit Jennifer's house and had no idea where it was.

Christine believes the Outback draws you back to visit, again and again. She also believes that, with a vivid imagination, you can travel anywhere.

www.audreyoftheoutback.net

Her shadow arms flailed on the bedroom wall.

One

Audrey dragged a cardigan over her night-gown. Her shadow arms flailed on the bedroom wall. The shadow was bigger than Audrey, as though it had grown without her. She didn't like looking at it and turned her back.

She wriggled her toes on the soft kangaroo-skin rug. Outside it would be cold and dark. Wind hissed dust against the wall, and the hessian curtain blew in. Everything would be coated with red dust in the morning. Earlier in the day, Audrey's dad reckoned he could smell rain coming. He had a pretty good nose for weather.

Audrey picked up her shoes, tipped them upside down and shook them. Centipedes played hide-and-seek in shoes, and they had too many legs and a nasty bite.

She wished she hadn't thought about centipedes, but now they were in her mind. Once you thought something, you couldn't *un*think it. You just had to wait for it to go away. Sometimes it was a long wait.

Audrey looked over at her little brother, Douglas, asleep in the other bed. His mouth hung open but, for once, he wasn't sucking his thumb.

She picked up the hurricane lamp from the chest of drawers. If she was quick, she'd soon be back in bed, warm and safe, under her grey blanket.

The logs in the sitting-room fireplace glowed red. Although the flames had died down hours ago, there was still a hint of wood smoke. As Audrey tiptoed past, a log cracked open, spitting red sparks. She jumped and shot into the small kitchen.

Her parents' bedroom door was closed. Mum was tired these days with that baby in her tummy. It must be like having a rabbit under her jumper. Dad reckoned Mum's tummy would get even bigger. After the baby arrived, where would all that stretched skin go? Audrey couldn't remember what Mum's tummy looked like after Douglas was born.

Audrey opened the kitchen door with her free hand. The wind whipped her long fair hair. Her unbuttoned cardigan flapped. She pulled one side over the other and pinned it in place with her left arm.

Holding out the lamp, she stepped outside. Something in the darkness rattled. Probably the chook pen. Dad kept repairing it, but it still shook when the wind blew.

Careful not to tilt the lamp, Audrey closed the door quietly behind her.

The goats and chooks were asleep. Audrey

felt as though she was the only person in the whole world who was awake. She beckoned to Stumpy. He didn't like walking about at night, but he came because he was her friend.

Clouds raced past the moon. The moonlight seemed to turn off and on. Then the sky was totally dark.

Audrey hurried towards the long-drop dunny.

'I hope there won't be any spiders,' she whispered to Stumpy. 'Price reckoned there was a *huge* one in there this morning.'

A howl rose above the wind.

Audrey shivered. 'I don't like the sound of dingoes, do you, Stumpy?'

Stumpy shook his head.

Then something moved down by the well.

Audrey stood perfectly still. 'Wh ... what's that?'

She peered into the darkness. The lamplight didn't go far and the wind made her eyes water. 'I saw something move. Fair dinkum, I did.'

She blinked dust from her eyes. Her heart pitter-pattered an urgent message: *go-back, go-back, go-back-inside*.

The clouds over the moon thinned. In the strange, weak light, she saw a pale shape hovering above the ground.

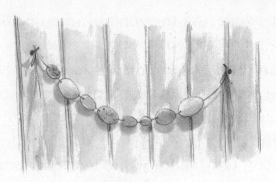

Two

'Price!' Audrey shoved open the door to her older brother's tiny bedroom at the side of the house. 'Wake up!'

A pool of light from the lamp showed Price's eyes were closed, and he was snoring.

Audrey moved closer and shook him.

The snoring stopped.

Price sat up. His hair stuck out like dry grass. 'Wassa matter?'

Audrey lifted the lamp.

He blinked at the sudden brightness.

'Something's outside,' whispered Audrey.

'It's dark and the wind's come up. What were you doin' out there?'

Audrey put her free hand on her hip. 'Checking the stars for twinkles.'

'Checking the . . . oh, you were going to the dunny.'

'I don't say *dunny*. I'm a lady now, since I went to Beltana. Ladies say *twinkle*.'

Price flopped back onto his pillow and closed his eyes.

Audrey grabbed his arm. 'I don't want to wake Mum. Get up. I saw something out the back. It was white and it moved. Down near the well.'

Price's eyes flicked open again. 'You're not pulling my leg, are you?'

Audrey shook her head.

Price threw back his blanket. His eggshell collection shook on its string. He swung his feet over the edge of the bed and stood up. His blue pyjama pants were too short and his ankles showed. 'Stay here.'

He headed for the door. As he opened it,

dust blew into his room. He slipped outside, and the door snapped shut.

Audrey lowered the lamp. Her arm was beginning to ache.

Minutes ticked by.

Maybe Price shouldn't be outside on his own.

He was taking a long time.

What if he was in trouble? If Price got eaten, it would be all her fault. She wasn't sure what would have a mouth big enough to munch a boy that size, but something strange was out there.

She charged across to the door and flung it open before she could think so much that her legs went wobbly.

Outside, the wind still hissed, but the dingo had stopped howling.

Audrey blinked dust from her eyes.

Where was Price?

Three

Audrey peered right, then left, trying to see through the cloud of dust.

She felt something land on her shoulder and squawked like a chook. She looked down and saw Price's hand. The lamp she was holding swung wildly.

'It's me, you dill!' Price curled his lip. 'Can't see nothin' but dust. Let's go inside.'

Audrey decided that a trip to the dunny could wait. She wasn't in that much of a hurry, and she was *not* going down there till it was light.

She put one finger to her lips to remind Price to be quiet, then they crept to her room. Stumpy had bolted for the bush when she ran to get Price, so there was no need to shush *him*.

Douglas had rolled over in his sleep and curled into a little ball. As he breathed, his nose gave a soft whistle.

'Quick, Audrey,' whispered Price. 'You're shivering.'

Audrey put the kerosene lamp on the chest of drawers and leapt into bed. She dragged the grey blanket up to her chin. 'Stay with me for a while?'

Price nodded.

'Can we leave the lamp on too?'

Price sat down on the kangaroo-skin rug. 'I'll tell you a story, if you want. How about *The Billy Goats Gruff*?'

'Are trolls real?' asked Audrey.

''Course not. You don't even know what a troll *is*.'

'Yes, I do. They live under bridges and

eat billy goats.' Audrey peered at her brother over the edge of the blanket. 'Why do trolls only eat boy goats and not girl goats? I bet boy goats are tough.'

'Do you want a story or not?' Price's voice rose to a louder whisper.

'I can listen and think questions at the same time.'

'Well, *I* can't.'

'That's because you're a boy. You'd be tough to eat too.'

Price sighed. 'Once upon a time . . .'

'*What* time?

'I don't know. *Any* time. It's the story that's important. Not *when* it happened.'

When a story took place *was* important. What if the billy goat had walked over the bridge a day earlier? The troll might have been on the other side of the mountain. He wouldn't have been there to say, 'Who's that walking on my bridge?' The goat would have skipped safely over the bridge and played with his friends.

'Once upon a time . . .'

'Price,' whispered Audrey. 'What did you really see out the back?'

'Not much. Just the same old things— vegetable patch, dunny, chookyard, the woodpile, goats . . . nothing else.'

But there *was* something else out there that Price didn't mention.

Graves.

Four

The next morning Audrey sat outside on a kerosene tin, one leg crossed over the other, her chin resting on her hands.

Last night's dust had been dampened down by a shower of rain. Dad's weather-nose had been right. The rain had also smoothed out footprints and other marks in the dirt. Not that Audrey had expected any. The kind of visitor she'd seen last night would not leave footprints. But she'd looked around, just to be sure.

She stared at the two wooden crosses.

Each one had writing on it. One said, 'Esther—three days' and the other, 'Pearl—two years'.

Audrey was glad her sisters were close by.

She'd seen their baby clothes in the big chest in Mum's bedroom. What would Pearl and Esther be like, if they'd lived? They were born before her, so they'd be older. Would they have told her what to do, or looked after her?

Maybe they would've seen Stumpy too. But no one could see unless they believed. Stumpy understood that, so he didn't mind. He was pretty smart for a camel.

Esther was a name that made Audrey think of a pretty girl in a frilly dress, who had a high voice and liked games. And she'd say 'Aud' not Audrey, because she'd be the kind of girl who showed she liked you by mucking about with your name. Price would be 'Pricey'. Audrey smiled to herself. Price would hate that. But Esther would use it anyway.

Pearl's name was short. 'No-nonsense', as old Mrs Paterson would say. Audrey imagined Pearl baking bread. The tops of the loaves would rise high over the tin. The bread would be crunchy on the outside, but soft and steaming inside. Pearl would be taller than anyone in the family, except Dad. Little girls wouldn't be scared if Pearl was around.

Audrey heard a familiar sound behind her. Dad was clearing his throat. He did that when he was getting ready to say something important.

'Two-Bob.' Dad squatted down on his heels beside her. There were wrinkles around his eyes, and his beard was bushier than ever.

'Good morning, Reginald.'

Dad raised one eyebrow. 'Even your mother doesn't call me *Reginald*. For however long this interest of yours in first names continues, Chip will suit me just fine. *Reginald* makes me think I'm in more trouble than a one-legged frog in a snake-pit. Besides, it's an old man's name.'

Audrey studied the deep lines around Dad's eyes. He got the lines by squinting against the sun when he was out bush. Judging by the amount of wrinkles, he'd been squinting for a lot of years.

'Did you make these crosses for the girls, Dad?'

He nodded.

The arms on the crosses were not quite straight. It wasn't the first time Audrey wondered if her dad needed glasses.

She looked out across the saltbush and red sand to the line of trees where the scrub began. 'Do you think people can come back from the other side?'

'The other side of what?'

'The other side of being alive.'

Dad cleared his throat again.

'Do you think Pearl and Esther are alive somewhere, Dad? But different to us?'

'I'm not sure, Audrey. But I miss them.'

'Me too. I didn't know them really, but they're still my sisters, aren't they? So that means I *do* know them even though I don't. Sort of.'

Dad scratched at his beard.

'If people *could* visit from that other place,' said Audrey, 'Do you think Pearl and Esther would try to see us?'

'If they could.'

'Would you be scared?'

'Of Pearl and Esther? Not on your life.' Dad looked at her from under bushy eyebrows. 'Why are you asking me these questions?'

'I saw something out here last night and it was sort of white like an angel dress.'

'You think an angel was out here?'

'Maybe not. She'd get her dress dirty walking around in the bush. And if I was an angel with wings, I wouldn't walk. I'd fly. Really fast.'

'That's a good point. Besides, if your sisters came back to visit, I reckon they'd go in the house. They wouldn't stay out here by the chookyard.'

'The chookyard smells, doesn't it, Dad?'

'When people dillydally with their chores and the manure piles up, yes it does.'

Audrey looked down at the ground. 'People in this family do their chores. It just takes a while sometimes.'

'*Mmm.*'

'Will you tell me more about Pearl and Esther?'

'Reckon I will,' said Dad. 'One day.'

Five

Audrey picked up a plate and began drying it with a cloth. Although the plate had a small chip in it, she was extra careful. This plate with the green bamboo pattern was her mum's favourite.

She looked out the kitchen window. Dad was using a stick to beat dust from kangaroo-skin rugs that hung from the clothes line. Mum was talking as she pointed to the rugs. Audrey expected Mum liked to help, although Dad couldn't miss with a stick that size.

Mum rubbed her tummy with one hand. She did that a lot lately. Maybe she was saying hello to the baby. Audrey wondered if the baby could feel it.

Douglas sat near the clothes line, playing in the dirt.

The kitchen door swung back against the wall with a bang. Price struggled in with both arms filled with wood for the sitting-room fire. His face was pink. As usual, he'd tried to shorten the number of trips by carrying too much. He couldn't unload the logs without dropping some.

'Want me to help you?' asked Audrey.

'Too right.' Price's voice sounded tight. He was concentrating hard on keeping the firewood in his arms.

Audrey put down the cloth and the plate and followed him into the sitting room.

Mum's sewing box sat on her favourite armchair. She was fixing up one of Dad's old shirts so Price could wear it. Price seemed to grow taller every day. Audrey wondered if his legs and arms creaked at night, like wood when the temperature changed.

Audrey looped her thick plaits together at the back of her neck, so they wouldn't swing forward and get in the way.

One by one, she took the logs and began stacking them in a neat pile beside the fireplace. They weren't too heavy, but she moved slowly. A few months back, she had dropped a piece of wood on her toe. She'd screamed so loudly that Price reckoned she popped his eardrums. Her toenail went black and came off. 'Well your toe's not so good,' Dad had said at the time, 'But there's nothing wrong with your lungs.'

Audrey was glad she hadn't screamed last night when she saw the white thing down near the well.

'Price, do you reckon wells are as good as billabongs?'

'Depends how deep the well is and how much water is in the billabong.'

'Do you think a deep well is better than a dry billabong?'

'If you want water.'

A log slipped from Audrey's fingers. She felt it falling and jumped back. It missed her feet, hit the floor and rolled to one side. The log didn't mark the floor. Crushed ants' nest and mud made a firm surface. The only time the floor cracked was if it dried out in the heat of summer.

Audrey stooped to pick up the log. 'What if you were a bunyip, Price?'

'I'm *not* a bunyip.'

'But what if you were? Do you reckon you'd like wells as much as billabongs?'

'Audrey, these questions are silly.'

'Not if you're a bunyip.'

'I *told* you. I'm *not* a bunyip. I'm a man.'

'You're a *boy*. You're too young to be a man.'

'I'm a *young* man.'

Audrey couldn't quite see how her brother could turn into a man—even a *young* man—in one night. Last December he'd gone to bed, eleven years old and a boy. Next morning, on his twelfth birthday, he started saying he was a man.

Audrey picked at a splinter that had speared her right thumb. 'But do you think a bunyip, even if it wasn't you, would like a well as much as a billabong?'

Price shook his head.

'Have you ever seen a bunyip, Price?'

He gave a little snort.

'Heard a bunyip growl?'

'I've heard some strange things in the bush.'

'Were they *bunyip* strange?' asked Audrey.

'Bunyips aren't real.'

'How do you know if you're *not* one and you haven't seen one?'

He opened his mouth, then closed it again. He'd catch flies if he kept flapping his jaw like that.

'You do know what bunyips look like, though,' said Audrey.

'I've told you before.'

'Tell me *again*.'

'They're huge and hairy, with red eyes on the sides of their heads, and fangs. They like water. They bellow at night. And they eat kangaroos and people.' Price lowered his voice, 'Especially women and girls.'

'I told you boys and billy goats were tough meat.' Audrey looked at her brother sideways. 'You know a lot about bunyips for someone who hasn't seen one and doesn't believe in them.'

Was that thing she'd seen last night a bunyip looking for water? It *had* been down near the well.

What if it was looking for something yummy to eat? Something wearing a night-gown and a cardigan. Audrey remembered the howling she'd heard. It had sounded like dingoes. But bunyips made noises too.

Audrey hadn't seen red eyes though. And a hungry bunyip would have eaten her right up when she was out there alone.

No, it couldn't have been a bunyip. Nor could it have been an angel. An angel would fly, and if Pearl and Esther came back to visit, they'd come inside the house.

But whatever it was, it was real. And Audrey knew she wouldn't stop thinking about it until she solved the mystery.

Had something moved out there?

Six

Back in the kitchen, Audrey wiped the last saucepan and hung it on its hook over the kitchen fireplace.

Next time Dad went south to Beltana, he was picking up a proper stove from Mrs Paterson. That stove would be the sort you put wood inside, behind a metal door. With one of those, Mum could cook bread and scones in the house. Although Dad had done a pretty good job of the bread oven out the back. It was made from crushed ants' nest and wire, and hardly crooked at all. Maybe his eyes had been better then.

Audrey glanced out of the window. A pleasant breeze drifted in. Most of last night's clouds had floated away and the sky was a deep blue.

Suddenly Audrey stood still and narrowed her eyes. Had something moved out there?

If so, it wasn't Stumpy. Today, he was playing out bush. He didn't like chores. And he wasn't that good at them either. Four legs weren't much use if you had to dry dishes or clean lamp glass with salt. You needed hands.

Audrey stood at the window, staring out.

When their dog, Grease, was alive, he had barked if a stranger showed up. He'd barked *too* much, actually, and he used to dig holes all around the house. He died just before the family went to Beltana, and Audrey missed him. Dad probably missed him even more. Grease used to go with him when he went away.

There! Audrey was certain now. A small

black dot moved on the edge of the tree line.

She ran to the door, wrenched it open and dashed towards the clothes line. 'Mum! Dad! Someone's coming.'

'Where?' Mum spun round, towards the track that led to their house. 'I can't see anything.'

'You will in a minute.'

Price leant the axe handle against the wall and dusted his hands.

Douglas forgot the game he was playing in the dirt with two sticks and jumped to his feet. 'I wannaseetoo.'

'Audrey, this isn't one of your make-believe stories, is it?' asked Mum.

'I don't make-believe things.'

'What about Stumpy?' Price wiped his forehead with his sleeve. The cuff flapped open. Either the button had gone missing or he hadn't bothered to do it up.

'He doesn't make up things neither.'

'No. I mean *you* made up *Stumpy*.'

Audrey felt sorry for her older brother. He couldn't see things since he'd grown taller and moved into his lean-to room at the side of the house. He was so busy growing that wishing and playing were being left behind.

'Stumpy is *real*,' she said in her firm-but-polite voice. The one she'd learned from Mrs Paterson. 'I see things that other people don't.'

'My oath, you do, Two-Bob.' Dad dropped the stick onto the ground. The kangaroo skins hung straight on the line.

'Wotisit? Wotisit?' A dirt smear curved from Douglas's nose across his left cheek. The knees of his trousers had round patches of dirt on them.

Dad smiled at Douglas. 'Someone's coming, all right.'

'I saw him first,' said Audrey. 'Cos I used Dad's wrinkles.'

'You did what?' Mum frowned and laughed at the same time.

'Like this.' Audrey squeezed up the skin

around her eyes to form a tight squint. 'Dad does this in the bush so he can see better. That's how he got his wrinkles. Us Barlows have bush eyes, don't we, Dad ... I mean, Chip?'

'Reckon so.'

Douglas ran to stand behind Mum's skirt. He leaned to one side, so he could still see the track.

The figure on the track seemed to grow larger as he came closer. He was solidly built and wore a broad-brimmed hat. A swag was slung over his back. His steps were slow and plodding. He'd probably walked a long way. If you set out too fast, you didn't get far because you felt tired before you reached the place you were going. 'One foot after the other will get you there,' Dad sometimes said when Audrey was rushing about, knocking into things.

Excitement gripped Audrey like a giant cramp. Even her fingers tingled. She danced up and down, then ran towards the visitor.

Seven

Up close, Audrey saw this was no ordinary swaggie.

He was a *she*. But she looked as tough as boots. She wore thick trousers and a baggy grey shirt. Her eyebrows were unusually pale. Much paler than the brown hair that showed beneath her hat. The swaggie was broad as well as tall, and her hands were rough and tanned.

Audrey had a feeling she'd seen this face and solid shape before.

The swaggie tilted back her head and

grinned at Audrey. Pink gums glistened in the sunlight. 'What d'ya know?'

Those bare gums and booming voice could only belong to one person. 'You're Bloke!'

'Blow me down. You know who I am?'

Audrey's smile was so wide that she felt her ears move. 'You gave me my other name, Two-Bob. You said I was as crazy as a two-bob watch.'

'Right on the nose.' Bloke chuckled and her whole body shook. She slapped Audrey on the back.

Audrey staggered. A pat like that could knock a person into next week.

'You remember me calling you Two-Bob?' Bloke's pale eyebrows danced up and down.

'Sort of. Dad told me about it too. He calls me Two-Bob a lot. I call *him* Reginald some-times.' Audrey fiddled with her plaits. 'He doesn't like that name too much.'

'Sounds like a gent who sits straight and folds his hands a lot.'

Audrey nodded. 'And a Reginald would always have clean fingernails. Dad doesn't. His are brown, even after he washes them. And when he's home, he baths every week. So I reckon his fingernails will be brown forever.'

She waved to her family, waiting by the clothes line.

Mum waved back.

'I reckon I saw one of those two-bob watches in Beltana. Actually, it wasn't a watch. It was a clock, which is bigger. It had dead Rome language numbers on it,' Audrey told Bloke. 'You came on a good day. Dad's going to make one of his rabbit stews in the big pot. We like his stews. Except Dad lets them boil too long and the vegetables get all broken and mash up with each other and you can hardly tell which one you're eating.'

Audrey skipped alongside Bloke's plodding feet. 'Dad's giving Mum a rest because she's got a baby in her tummy. I want a girl. But Dougie, my little brother, wants a horse. Dougie's only three, so his brain's not working all that good yet. When he felt the baby kicking in Mum's tummy, he cried because he thought she'd eaten it.'

'It's all comin' back to me now, why I called you Two-Bob.'

Audrey giggled.

'You've gone and grown on me,' said Bloke. 'I remember you bein' knee-high to a grasshopper.'

If she ever shouted, Bloke could blow kookaburras out of trees. Maybe when people had no teeth, there was nothing to dampen the sound of their voice.

'I got trousers too, like you.' Audrey plucked at her braces, then let them snap back. 'I have to roll up the cuffs. They're too long because they were my brother's. But girls can wear trousers.'

'Too right we can.'

'We can't grow beards though.'

Bloke guffawed. 'Suits me just fine, I can

tell you. Some of them blokes on the track got more wildlife in their beards than there is in the zoo.'

'Is that why men scratch their beards a lot?'

'Could be.'

As they passed the new dunny with real walls, Audrey called out, 'Chip! Everhilda! It's Bloke! The girl swaggie.'

Bloke stepped forward and offered her hand to Dad. He didn't often shake hands with girls or women. Bloke squeezed his hand up and down as though it were a pump handle. If Bloke shook hands with the same strength that she slapped backs, then it had to hurt. But Dad didn't even wince.

'Bwoke,' called Douglas, from behind Mum's skirts.

Bloke didn't shake Mum's hand, but she showed her gums in a wide smile. 'Mrs B,' said Bloke, and tipped her hat just as a man would do.

Price said, 'Hello'. But he stayed back near the house. Which was good because he was as skinny as a greyhound. If Bloke shook hands with Price, she'd probably lift him right off the ground.

'Did you visit us last night?' Audrey asked Bloke.

Bloke shook her head. 'Been walkin' since sun-up. I was miles away last night. Couldn't see the hand in front of me face in that dust storm. I stayed put till it passed.' She took off her hat and wiped sweat from her face with her left forearm. Her brown hair was flattened and there was a red line across her forehead from her hatband. 'And there's not much chance of a cuppa if you turn up at night.'

The mystery of the moving shape in the darkness was still alive.

'You behave yourself, mate.'

Eight

Audrey held out the tin. Bloke carefully placed an egg in it, then added a second and a third.

Suspicious of the big black rooster, Audrey kept her eyes on him. 'Watch out for Nimrod. He's started flying up at people. He doesn't like anyone taking the eggs.'

Bloke grunted and kept searching the ground. The hens had little wooden boxes they were supposed to lay eggs in, but sometimes they dropped them in the yard. Audrey wondered why the eggs didn't break when they fell out. It could be because chook bottoms weren't that far off the ground.

'It's a good thing eggs aren't round like cricket balls,' said Audrey. 'Otherwise they'd bounce.'

'You might be right.' Bloke squatted on her heels and eyeballed the big rooster. 'You behave yourself, mate.'

He stared back at her with beady chook eyes. Then he moved his little head backwards and forwards as though he was showing off. Audrey wondered if the girl chooks minded that he was so bossy. But he was looking after them all right. They hadn't been eaten by foxes or dingoes.

Bloke dusted her hands and stood up.

From the back of the house came the steady crack of an axe splitting wood. Without even looking, Audrey could tell it was her dad. When Price was cutting wood it was: *chop*, *chop*, stop, *chop*. Followed by muttering and, sometimes, a yelp.

Over in the other pen, Sassafras bleated.

'Do you reckon goats sound like babies crying?' Audrey asked Bloke.

'Haven't had much to do with babies. But it's hard to ignore a goat.'

'Do you think they smell funny?'

'I've smelled worse things.' Bloke gave a lopsided grin. 'Includin' meself.'

'What's white and sort of floats in the air?' asked Audrey.

Bloke put a fourth egg into the tin. Her lips looked dry and flaky. Audrey guessed she didn't wear her hat all the time and the sun had dried out her skin.

'Is this a riddle?'

'No. I saw something last night, down by the well.' Audrey peeked up at Bloke from beneath her eyelashes. She hoped Bloke wouldn't laugh at her question.

'I've seen lots of strange things in the bush.'

'Price says that too. But he never tells me *what*.'

'That thing you saw,' said Bloke. 'Could be a min min light.'

'What's that?'

'A light in the bush. They're mostly seen at night.'

Audrey felt the hairs on the back of her neck stand up. 'Have you ever seen a min min light?'

'Once. In New South Wales.'

'What did it do?' whispered Audrey.

'It hovered, like this ...' Bloke held up her left hand and shook it like a leaf in the wind. 'It circled around and came at me real fast. Then it followed me.'

'What'd you do?'

'Walked a *lot* faster.'

'Did you try to catch it?'

Bloke grimaced. '*No*. If you chase a min min and catch it, you disappear.'

'Disappear?' Audrey's word ended on a squeak. She looked across at her sisters' wooden crosses. 'Do you know anyone who got dead by a min min light?'

'Not anyone I know. But I seen a couple of bodies in the bush, and I don't know how they ended up that way.'

'What are they really, those min min lights?'

'Can't be sure. But one old Aborigine bloke told me they were dead men's camp fires.'

A shiver ran down Audrey's spine. 'Do they get cold?'

'Who?'

'Dead men.'

'Maybe we shouldn't be talkin' about this.' It was Bloke's turn to shiver.

'Why not?'

'Don't open a door,' said Bloke, 'unless you want to see what's behind it.'

Nine

Bloke licked her lips, all round.

Audrey sneaked a look down the kitchen table at Price. He was staring at Bloke.

Mum and Dad forked through their rabbit stew without glancing up. That told Audrey that they, too, wanted to stare. But they were trying not to do it. No one liked rabbit stew so much they could forget about watching Bloke eat. Not even when it was Dad's stew.

Douglas tilted his head, his blue eyes wide with curiosity. 'Wheresyourteef?'

Mum tapped Douglas's arm.

Bloke curled her palms around her teacup, lifted it to her mouth and slurped the tea. Her meaty fingers made the teacup look too small. She certainly couldn't fit those fingers through the handle. She glanced up and saw everyone looking at her. 'Is he talkin' to me?'

'Where's your teef?' Douglas asked again, but slower this time.

Bloke set down her cup and laughed.

'Did the toof faiwy take dem?'

'He means *tooth fairy*,' Audrey explained. Her cheeks felt hot, and it wasn't just from the heat of the kitchen fire.

Bloke let loose another laugh. 'I'd be rich if I'd sold all me teeth to the tooth fairy. Anyways, don't reckon the ol' tooth fairy comes out this far.' She looked across the table at Douglas. 'Me teeth weren't no good to me. Kept hurting all the time. I pulled out a couple, then thought, heck, why not pull out the whole blinkin' lot.'

'You pulled them out *yourself*?' Price had a pink patch on each cheek that suggested he was also warm.

'Easy with plyers.' Bloke opened her mouth and put her finger on the lower jaw. 'Ha ... abi ... o ...' She pulled out her finger and wiped it on her sleeve. 'Had a bit of trouble with that back one. Roots were all twisted, see. Like this.' She curled her two forefingers around each other.

Mum coughed and stood up. Her face was as green as the cardigan she wore over her floral dress. 'Excuse me.' She pushed back her chair and dashed outside.

'Mum's in the expecting with the baby,' explained Audrey. 'So she spits up a lot.'

'Two-Bob.' Dad frowned. 'It's not good manners to talk about that at the table.'

'Sorry, Dad.'

It didn't seem nearly as bad as watching Bloke describe pulling out her teeth with plyers. But there were different rules for visitors. Down in Beltana, Mrs Paterson had so many rules about manners that she had lists and made children write them down.

Dad took a rabbit bone from his mouth with his thumb and forefinger. He looked at it for a moment, then dropped it on his bread-and-butter plate. 'Staying in these parts long, Bloke?'

Audrey wasn't sure if her dad really wanted to know or if he was trying to stop everyone talking about teeth-pulling.

'Few days. Till the wind changes.' Bloke folded her hands over her round tummy. Unlike Mum's tummy, there was no baby in there. But there was certainly a lot of stew. Bloke pushed it in fast because she didn't waste time chewing. She just sucked at the meat, bounced it around on her gums for a while, then swallowed.

Thinking of tummies made Audrey wonder when her mum would come back inside. Audrey's eyes slid towards the closed kitchen door.

Douglas patted the last of his stew with

his spoon. Gradually the pats became smacks. Drops of gravy splashed up onto his cheeks.

Dad reached over and took the spoon from him.

Outside, one of the camels bellowed. They were tethered away from the house, behind the vegetable patch. Had the camel bellowed because it was bored, or because it sensed something strange hiding in the darkness?

'Dad!' said Audrey, 'Someone should go and get Mum.'

Ten

Early the next day, Audrey strode out. She was determined to go all the way to her cubbyhouse. The bush seemed unusually quiet, the sky wider than it should be. Gum trees cast twisted shadows.

'It's all right, Stumpy,' she whispered. 'Monsters don't come out in the daytime.'

Audrey thrust both hands in the pockets of her oversized trousers. The fingers of her right hand closed around the boiled egg that her mum had given her. It was still warm.

As she thought of her mum, Audrey's

stomach tightened, just as it had last night when Mum was alone outside. She'd come back inside and told them all not to worry. But once people started worrying, it was hard to stop.

'Mum didn't see anything scary,' Audrey told Stumpy. 'But I did. I know I did.'

Stumpy told her that he believed her.

That made Audrey feel a little better.

'Let's be pirates today, Stumpy, then we can go to our cubby ship.'

Stumpy liked playing pirates.

Quandong seeds dangled on strings around her hat brim. They kept the flies away from her face.

Stumpy ran alongside her on the track. Spinifex and grey saltbush grew on each side of it.

A kangaroo bounded out of the trees. It stopped when it saw Audrey, twitched its ears, then took off in the other direction. Its tummy was fat and, just for a second, Audrey saw little feet sticking up from its pouch. She wondered if the joey got dizzy, hanging upside down, while its mother bounced.

Mum's baby was upside down too. When it kicked, the top of her tummy fluttered. So it must be standing on its head. But at least Mum didn't bounce like a kangaroo. She didn't even run.

At last, Audrey spied her cubby through the trees.

But as she came closer, her steps slowed. 'Stumpy! Something's wrong.'

Tingles ran from Audrey's neck down to her arms.

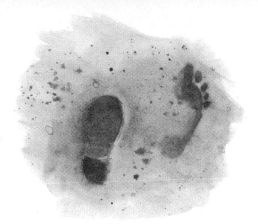

Eleven

'It's the door.' Audrey's voice was as soft as the faintest breeze.

Whenever she left her cubby, she dragged some brush in front of the opening. The branches were always at the top, with twigs and leaves at the bottom. At home, her family hung a branch upside down like that to show when someone was in the dunny. Now, her brush cubby-door was the other way round.

Audrey sneaked closer. Her heart beat faster.

She'd taken a lot of care building this cubby. The branches and leaves for the walls were as thick as she could stack them. It was half-round, like a giant ant hill.

Through the gaps in the leaves, Audrey spotted something lying on the ground inside the cubby. But she couldn't see clearly enough to know what it was. Her heart beat even louder. It echoed in her ears.

No animal could drag aside the brush door, go inside, then close it behind them. Even Stumpy would find that hard.

'That lump in there isn't moving,' she whispered. 'Reckon it's a swag?'

Stumpy didn't know.

'It's not *Bloke's* swag. Although she's only camped a mile away.'

Audrey looked down at the red sandy soil and saw footprints. One shoe print, and a bare footprint with little toe-marks. Audrey put her own foot next to the shoe print. Her boot-mark was slightly bigger. Whoever was in the cubby was a child.

Why didn't they call out? Were they sick? Or worse, what if they'd *died* in the cubby?

She wasn't sure whether to peek inside or run away.

Tingles ran from Audrey's neck down to her arms.

She couldn't leave someone in trouble.

'H . . . hello?' Her voice wobbled.

There was no answer.

Audrey clenched her fingers into fists at her side and swallowed hard. 'I'm coming in!'

Twelve

Audrey grabbed the brush door and dragged it back.

Inside the cubby, a girl sat up.

Audrey squeaked.

The girl stared at her. She was Aboriginal, with large brown eyes and short curly hair. Dressed in a pale smock-dress, she wore a fawn cardigan over the top. She had a small nose and thick eyelashes. The girl pulled in her bottom lip and pinned it with her front teeth.

'Hello,' said Audrey.

The girl said nothing.

'I'm Audrey Barlow. I live in the little house with the noisy goats over that way.' She waved one arm.

The girl looked past Audrey into the bush.

'I came to play.' Audrey took off her hat and held it with both hands. 'This is my cubbyhouse.'

Silence lay between them as thick as dripping on bread.

Maybe the girl didn't understand.

Audrey knew only two sorts of words: English and camel. Well, Stumpy camel, anyway. He understood everything she said. And much that she didn't. Maybe this girl had her own words for things.

They were a long way from any other houses. How did the girl get out here?

There was a brown lace-up shoe on her left foot, but not on her right. Her ankle was badly swollen. It looked like a paddymelon with a foot on the end of it.

'Oh, you've hurt yourself.' Audrey stepped towards the girl, squatted down beside her and dropped her hat on the ground.

Instinctively, the girl moved away. She whimpered, her eyes watering.

Once, Audrey had sprained her wrist sliding down a sandhill on a sheet of tin. She'd cried and cried. Even Mum's scones hadn't stopped her tears. The girl's puffy ankle would be just as painful. Her eyes were huge and she hardly blinked.

Audrey hesitated. She thought as hard as she could. But she didn't know what to do. The girl's ankle might be broken.

'I'll fetch my dad,' Audrey told her. 'He can help you.'

The girl's hands flew to her face. 'No! They'll get me.'

Thirteen

Audrey threw a look over her shoulder. Thoughts of min min lights and bunyips raced through her mind.

But all she saw was Stumpy. His long legs were trembling and his eyes were as wide as the girl's.

'*Who'll* get you?' Audrey asked.

A small silence stretched into a long one. Maybe the girl didn't want to talk about what scared her. Sometimes when you gave a name to something that frightened you, it came looking for you. Audrey remembered old Mrs Paterson saying, 'Speak of the Devil and in he walks.'

'You said words, so I know you can talk,' said Audrey.

'I talk good. All the time.'

'Me too. My dad says I could talk underwater with a mouth full of marbles. I don't know if that's true because our bath is so small my legs hang over the side.'

The girl glanced at Audrey, then away again.

'What's your name?'

'Janet.'

'I've got two names. Audrey and Two-Bob.'

'I got two names, too. Janet, that's the name *they* call me. My other name, my family gave me.'

'What is it?'

Janet beckoned Audrey closer.

Audrey crawled over. It was only a little way and the sandy soil was soft.

Janet leaned forward, put one hand up to Audrey's ear, and whispered. Then she sat back. 'No one can call me that name till I get back home. First person gonna say it again is my mum.'

'Your real name sounds nice,' said Audrey. 'How old are you?'

Janet shrugged.

'Don't you like to say how old you are?' Audrey crossed her legs and rested her elbows on her knees.

'Maybe this many.' Janet held up eight fingers. Then she held up seven, changed her mind and made it six.

Outside the cubbyhouse, a kookaburra called out. It sounded like loud laughter.

Instantly, Janet grabbed hold of Audrey's wrist and squeezed tight.

Audrey hardly dared to breathe.

Fourteen

Audrey hardly dared to breathe.

She listened for any sounds that didn't belong in the bush. Anything which might suggest someone was out there. But there was just the wind and the crows, then the kookaburra again.

Stumpy, his lower jaw moving from side to side, stood outside the doorway.

With her free hand, Audrey put one finger to her lips, reminding him to be quiet.

'Who's there?' hissed Janet.

'Just my camel. He's called Stumpy. I don't think anyone else is out there. Do you?'

Janet let go of Audrey's wrist and looked at the open doorway of the cubby. 'That camel, he your family?'

'He's my *friend*. He's got four legs and a big mouth. He doesn't spit though, and he doesn't smell like other camels. And he has beautiful big eyes. Most people can't see him.'

The two girls exchanged understanding looks.

'I reckon *you* could probably see him,' said Audrey. 'You've got the right sort of eyes.'

'He's yours. My family, we got kooka-burras.'

Audrey shifted and felt the boiled egg in her pocket. 'Are you hungry?'

Janet's eyes flashed.

Audrey reached into her pocket, took out the egg and offered it to her.

'Half each?' suggested Janet.

'I'm not hungry. You have it.' Audrey's stomach rumbled. She hoped Janet hadn't heard it.

Janet took the egg, smacked it between her hands, then peeled it. Pieces of white shell fell on the red sandy soil.

'What happened to your ankle?' asked Audrey.

'I was runnin' and my foot went down a rabbit hole.' Janet's face crinkled, as though she was going to cry. Instead, she pushed the egg into her mouth and began chewing. Yellow yolk-crumbs fell onto her dress. She picked them up between two fingertips, the way Douglas sometimes picked up ants. Then Janet put the crumbs in her mouth. That was also what Douglas did with ants.

'Men in a car, they takin' me from the mission down to Quorn. They said they'd give me lollies. They told me that before, long time ago, when they took me from my family, first time. But there's no lollies. They said they'd take me back home.' Janet had a faraway look, as though her eyes were seeing into forever. 'They never gonna do that.'

'What men?'

'Police, I reckon. They got buttons here.' Janet ran one finger from her neck down to her waist. 'Those men got bad faces.' She narrowed her eyes. 'When they first take me and the others, we hear those cars and we run. My mum hid me in the bush. But the men found me. I been at the mission, learning school things and washin' floors. Now they saying some woman in Quorn looking for a girl to work in her kitchen. Or wash clothes. Or somethin'. I don't care if it's kitchen or clothes. All the same to me. I don't want to go.'

Little girls helped their mums. But they didn't go out to work. At the Barlow house, Monday's washing was hard work. It took all day, even when there were several people to help. Audrey couldn't lift a wet sheet by herself. It was too heavy. Dad or

Price lifted the sheets now that Mum wasn't allowed, in case the baby didn't like it.

'Tyre on the car went *bang* when we were going to Quorn. They was tryin' to fix it and I ran into the bush.' Janet wiped the back of her hand across her mouth. One last yellow crumb fell. She pinched that up too and popped it in her mouth. 'Did all right till I twisted my ankle.'

'There's plenty of bushes around here to hide in,' suggested Audrey. 'And you can stay in my cubbyhouse until your ankle's better.'

'They might get a tracker. His eyes will be like an eagle's. Good tracker, he could tell those men how tall I am, if I'm carrying somethin', how long before I left foot marks in the sand.'

'My dad could . . .'

'*No.* Those men will make him give me back to them.' Janet's eyes widened. 'I'll never get home. My mum and my aunties, they calling my name every day. I hear them.'

Audrey felt hot stinging behind her eyes. It was horrible to even *think* about men with too many buttons snatching her away from her family. She imagined what it would be like, stuck in the bush with an empty stomach and a swollen ankle.

'I'm goin' *home*.' Janet's eyes flashed again.

Audrey believed her. A girl with eyes like that could do anything. Audrey looked down at Janet's puffy ankle. Janet's heart was bursting to get home, but her leg might not let her.

'I'll lean on a stick,' said Janet.

'That's a good idea. But your ankle will have to get a bit better before you can use a walking stick.'

Janet's face fell.

'We've got a billycart at home!' said Audrey. 'Dad made it and it even works. It's wood and it's got wheels. There's a rope on the front for pulling it. You could use that and you wouldn't have to walk.'

Janet thought for a moment. 'But who's gonna pull that rope?'

'Oh.' Audrey blew air into her cheeks. 'I forgot about that. And sometimes, if the sand is soft, the wheels get stuck.'

'I'll have to walk. Unless I ride an emu.' Janet chuckled.

'Wouldn't you be scared?'

'I could hang on to his feathers.'

Audrey nodded. 'It'd be hard getting him to stand still while you climb on though. Our camels hate it, even though Dad rides them all the time and he's got a saddle . . .'

Hope shone in Janet's eyes.

Audrey spoke first, 'A *camel* . . . you could borrow one of Dad's camels.'

Then Janet's shoulders slumped. 'Can't tell your dad about me.'

'But Dad's a nice man . . .'

'No!' Janet's eyes widened. 'Grown-up people bring back other kids that run away. I seen it lots of times. Always, they bring 'em back. Those kids cryin' when they come back . . . and they don't go out again.'

Audrey stopped arguing. Janet's mind was made up. There was no changing it. 'We can't borrow a camel without telling him.'

'I'm gonna *walk*, soon as I can. Got here, didn't I?' Janet shook her head.'Promise you won't tell about me?'

'I promise.'

It was one thing to say that. But keeping Janet a secret from Audrey's family would be much harder.

Fifteen

'Audrey!'

She flinched and looked up, her pulse racing.

Her mum stood at the corner of the house, a bucket of water in her hand. She leaned slightly to one side. Either the bucket was heavy or her gammy leg was playing up.

'Are you all right, dear?'

'Mum! You scared me.'

'I'm didn't mean to. I'm sorry. You look as white as a sheet. Are you feeling sick?'

Mum's face didn't have much colour either.

Audrey bounded towards her. 'I was thinking and my head was loud. I didn't hear you coming. Dad said you shouldn't carry heavy buckets.' She grabbed the handle of the bucket. 'I'll help, then we're only doing half each.'

She thought of Janet, offering to share half of the egg.

Mum smiled and her eyes crinkled. It was a nice crinkling though. Mum had pretty eyes. Audrey's eyes were the same colour, but she didn't think she'd ever be as pretty as Mum. Audrey wondered if Janet looked like *her* mum.

As they stepped out together, water slopped over the top of the bucket.

'Let's slow down, shall we?' said Mum. 'We're not on our way to a fire.'

Audrey matched her steps to her mum's. The bucket wasn't big, but the handle dug into Audrey's palm. Water was tricky. You could see right through it, but it was as heavy as anything.

'Your dad and Price have gone looking for the camels.' Mum sighed. 'They got loose again.'

Audrey felt her back stiffen. What if the camels ran towards her cubby, and her dad and Price saw Janet? Janet might think Audrey had broken her promise and told her family she was there. What would happen to Janet then?

'I don't know why we bother tethering the camels,' said Mum.

Crow noises from inside the house told Audrey that Douglas had woken from his afternoon nap.

Audrey and her mum stopped at the kitchen door. It was only wide enough for one person to enter at a time.

'I'm big enough to lift the bucket inside.' Audrey tried to make her voice firm. The way Dad sometimes did when his mind was made up. But it didn't come out that way.

Audrey simply sounded as though she had a sore throat.

Mum let go of the bucket and held open the kitchen door.

The bucket of water pulled on Audrey's arms and neck. The handle dug further into her palms. If Janet had to work in some woman's kitchen, she might be carrying many heavy buckets like this.

Audrey made it into the kitchen, spilling only a few drops.

'Leave the bucket on the floor. Dad can lift it up onto the table when he gets back,' said Mum.

Audrey rubbed at her palms, but the red handle-lines stayed on her skin.

'Cuppa?' Mum picked the billy up from the bench. 'I'm as dry as a bone.'

'Can we have bread too, with lots of jam?'

'You must have walked a long way today,' said Mum.

Audrey shrugged. If she folded a slice of

bread in half, it would slip into a pocket very nicely. Most likely, she could fit in two slices, one each side.

The Douglas-crow noises up in the bedroom stopped.

Audrey took the billy from her mum and slipped the ladle from its hook on the wall. 'Mum, if I got taken away from you, would you call my name every day?'

Her mum leaned back against the table, her hand against her chest. 'If you weren't here, I'd think about you all the time.'

Audrey scooped water from the bucket into the billy. Drips dotted the mud floor. The billy wouldn't take long to boil once it was hung over the fire.

'Do you think I'd know if you were calling me?' asked Audrey.

Mum came over and put her arms around Audrey's shoulders and hugged her. It was a sideways hug. It was getting harder to get close to Mum front-ways. Her tummy got in the way.

'I believe you *would* know.'

'Can I ask you a question about Pearl and Esther?' Audrey stayed with her face against her mother.

'Of course you can.' Mum's voice seemed to come from a long way above Audrey.

'Do you call *their* names?'

'Every day.' Mum's voice sounded thick. 'But inside.'

'Why do you do it *inside*?' Audrey kept her arms firmly around her mother's large waist.

'My granny used to say, "Laugh and the world laughs with you. Cry, and you cry alone."'

'But if you cry alone, then no one can help you.' Audrey looked up then.

Her mum's eyes were moist and shiny.

'I'm never going to get married,' said Audrey. 'I'm going to stay with you forever.'

Mum patted her back.

'Anyways, if I got married, I'd have to get used to a lot of beard scratching. Bloke reckons men have got animals in there. Real little ones.'

Mum made a hiccup sound. 'Don't ever change, Audrey Barlow.'

It was too late for that. Audrey couldn't remember keeping a secret from her mum before. She wanted to tell her all about Janet, but she couldn't. And that changed everything.

Sixteen

Audrey parted the hessian curtains in her bedroom, held out the potato bag and let it drop outside.

'Mind that, Stumpy,' she whispered. 'I'll be round to get it in a minute.

She turned to find Douglas staring up at her, his blue eyes intense. He had his sneaky slippers on. Made of kangaroo skin, they muffled the sound of his footsteps.

'Wanna come wiv you.' He rocked back and forth on his feet.

'Who said I was going anywhere?'

Usually, she didn't mind him tagging along. But today she had plans that could not include him. He didn't understand secrets. If he heard something, it went from his ears to his mouth in a few seconds.

'Come *wiv* you.'

'Not this time,' said Audrey. 'I have to run, and your legs are short.'

'Cawwie me.'

'You're too heavy. I can't carry you. It's a long way. I'm going to ask Bloke to come across for tea tonight. You can see her then.'

Douglas pouted.

Audrey hoped he wasn't about to have a tantrum. Mum would ask her to take him along.

'I'll play a game with you when I get back.' Audrey smiled.

Douglas nodded. His hair was still messy from his afternoon rest, and dried jam smeared his right cheek.

The clanging and banging of pots from the kitchen told Audrey that her mum was preparing preserved meat for tonight's tea. It took hours to soak out the extra salt before it could be cooked.

'Wanna *come too*,' demanded Douglas.

Audrey hesitated. She'd planned to drop the bag of food outside the window, walk out the back door, then sneak around to pick it up. If she waltzed past her mum with a bag over her shoulder, there'd be questions. Audrey didn't want to tell a fib. *Not* telling about Janet was different to making up stories.

Janet had eaten only one boiled egg in a couple of days. Her cardigan was thin and the nights were cold at this time of year. Audrey imagined Janet, trying to hobble a few steps, her ankle hurting, stomach rumbling, and listening for people hunting her.

Douglas glared at Audrey.

He didn't fuss that often. But when he did, his face went redder than a summer sunset and he was loud. Today he was probably tired. He'd spent his rest time making bird calls rather than sleeping. When he was tired, he was *extra* loud.

Audrey knelt in front of Douglas. 'When you go for a walk, you should wear your boots. Otherwise your feet will get sore and you might tread on a three-cornered jack.'

His pout turned into a smile. 'Boots.'

'That's right.'

Douglas ran through the sitting room into the kitchen. 'Mumwheresmyboots?'

'What did you say, dear?' Audrey heard her mum say. 'Slow down.'

Audrey hooked one leg over the window-sill. She heaved her body up and over, landing in the sandy soil outside.

'Sorry, Dougie,' she whispered.

Grabbing the bag, she lifted it and slung it over one shoulder so it rested there. 'Let's go,' she told Stumpy. 'Quick!'

She jogged into the bush, with the bag bouncing on her back.

A howl came from the house behind her.

That was a 'Dougie howl' all right. It was almost as bad as a dingo's.

Audrey's stomach tightened.

'Yes, I know Dougie's upset. I can hear him. And don't look at me like that,' she told Stumpy. 'You know *what* look. The one you're doing now. It wasn't *exactly* a fib. It's *true* that you need boots if you're going to walk in the bush. And I didn't say in words that I'd take him.'

Douglas had thought that on his own. She'd simply let him. Yet her stomach was twisting and turning like an angry snake. Douglas had trusted her. He had run off, all smiles, to get his little boots.

She rolled the tip of her tongue against her top lip to see if she could feel a pimple. Mrs Paterson said that people who told lies got pimples on their tongue.

Already, keeping Janet a secret was hard. Even if Audrey didn't speak about it, she could hear the whispers in her mind. And they wouldn't stop.

Seventeen

Janet stared hungrily at Audrey's potato bag.

Audrey dug in her right pocket and pulled out a thick slice of bread. Folded in half, it had red plum jam squeezing out of it. 'Sorry, it got squished.'

She peeked at Janet's ankle. It was still swollen. But Audrey didn't say anything about it. Janet might get upset.

Janet took three bites of the bread before she stopped to chew. 'Good tucker. Better than that porridge at the mission. Got no taste.'

The bread in Janet's mouth distorted her words. But Audrey understood. She'd had lots of practice working out what Douglas was saying. Audrey felt a hot pang in her chest as she pictured her little brother's blue eyes looking up at her.

'Do you have porridge back home, with your family?' asked Audrey.

Janet shook her head vigorously and swallowed. 'My best thing to eat is witchetty grubs. They taste real good. Mum and me and my aunties, we look for cracks in the ground, under a tree. Then we dig up a fat tree root with our sticks and break it to get the witchetty. Gotta be careful, though. Hit that root too hard and you squash the witchetty grub.'

'What do they taste like?' Audrey slid the second slice of bread from her other pocket and handed that over as well.

'Eggs, I reckon. If you cook them, they crunchy outside.'

Audrey wasn't sure she'd like witchetty

grubs. Although her dad had eaten tadpoles. Witchetty grubs couldn't be worse than that. If Janet could eat mission porridge, then Audrey could eat a witchetty grub. Especially if you could put jam on it. Jam made things taste sweet.

She reached inside the bag again and took out a brown-paper parcel. 'There's half a cooked rabbit in here. Not much meat on it. But you could suck the bones the way Bloke does. She's got no teeth but she leaves the bones so clean you'd think she'd scrubbed them.'

Janet put the parcel on the ground beside her. Her mouth was still full of bread.

'I brought you dried apricots, a cold baked potato, and a tin of jam.' Audrey sighed. 'I forgot about opening the tin, though.'

'Smash it with a rock.'

Audrey held up the red cardigan that Mrs Paterson had knitted especially for her. The sleeves were too long, but the old lady thought it was better to have things bigger than you needed. 'You can borrow this till you leave,' Audrey said, feeling a tug of uncertainty about lending her favourite cardigan. But Janet needed to keep warm. And the wool cardigan was thick and soft.

'I brought you pencils and a book to write in. For when you're resting your ankle,' said Audrey. She thought it was better not to say that Janet's ankle might not let her leave for some days. Janet had spent lots of hours out here alone and she had probably been worrying.

'My cousin, Jimmy, sent the pencils and book from the city,' Audrey said.

'Me, I got forty couthins.'

Audrey giggled. No one could have *that* many cousins. Janet must've got her numbers mixed up.

'That other tin has a lid you can lift off, and it's got water in it,' said Audrey. 'I'll try to bring you some more food tomorrow. But it's hard sneaking things out of the kitchen.'

'You lucky you got that camel watchin' out for you.'

Audrey looked through the opening. Stumpy stood outside, eating grass.

'Can you see him too?'

'I know he's out there. Same way I know my family's calling me.'

'My mum calls my two sisters, but no one else can hear. Just them. My sisters died. They're resting out the back of our place so they don't get lonely.'

'Your mum. My mum. Same voice, I reckon. It's loud even when they sayin' nothing.'

'Too right,' said Audrey. 'Think we'll have a voice like that when we're mums?'

'Maybe.' Janet grabbed a handful of dried apricots from their paper wrapping and slipped them, one at a time, into her mouth. She was slowing down after all that bread. 'But if you're a mum then you gotta have a man who's dad. Men spit and they have to go huntin'.'

'And they scratch their beards.'

Both girls nodded thoughtfully.

'Even if we're not mums when we grow up, we can be friends,' said Audrey.

'With each other?' Janet fiddled with her next apricot. 'Me and you?'

'We're friends *now*.'

'I haven't had no friend like *you* before.'

'Like what?'

'You got a camel in your family.'

'I haven't had no friend like you before.'

Eighteen

Standing on top of the termite mound made Audrey feel tall. She looked down at Bloke's neatly rolled swag lying near a circle of small rocks. Ash and sand inside the circle showed that was where Bloke had lit her camp fire.

'Bloke knows what she's doing,' Audrey told Stumpy. 'She covered the hot ash with sand to put out the fire.'

Stumpy thought that was a good thing too. He was scared of fire.

'I wonder where she is?' A feeling of

unease wrapped around Audrey like a shawl. Through the trees, not such a long walk away, Janet was hiding in the cubby-house.

Audrey leapt off the termite mound. Her feet made a *paff* sound as they hit the ground. The mound was taller than Audrey. It looked like giant dollops of grainy scone-dough, but it was as hard as rock.

One hand cupped around her mouth, she called, 'Cooee'.

A flock of cockatoos, their wings white against the green leaves, rose squawking from a tree.

An answering 'cooee' came from the bush to Audrey's left.

'It's all right, Stumpy. Bloke's gone the other way.'

The empty potato-bag clasped in her right hand, Audrey marched towards the sound of Bloke's call. Audrey was careful where she put her feet. She didn't want to step in a rabbit hole like Janet had. And snakes didn't always pay attention to the seasons. Some of them went out for a wriggle any old time.

Bloke held a small axe in one hand and a billy can in the other. She wore the same dusty trousers and laced boots as yesterday. Her brown shirt was much cleaner than the grey one, but it smelled of wood smoke. Audrey figured Bloke had eaten her breakfast on the smoky side of her camp fire. Although Audrey had heard her dad say, more than once, that camp fire smoke would find you wherever you stood.

'I'm gettin' some bush honey.' Bloke's eyes drifted to the empty bag in Audrey's hand. 'You gonna catch something in that?'

'Um ...' Audrey's thoughts fluttered like a moth around a light. 'It's a bag.'

Bloke raised one eyebrow. 'Yeah, *I* reckon it is too.'

Audrey couldn't explain the real reason she was carrying the bag and it was hard to think of another one quickly. 'Er ... I expectionate I might see something that I didn't know would be there. That's why I wouldn't know, because I haven't seen it yet.'

Bloke stared at Audrey. 'You like curly words, don't you?'

Audrey sighed. It would've been much easier to tell the truth.

'The honey isn't far. Come on.' Bloke turned and began to walk.

Audrey followed her, relieved that Bloke had stopped asking about her empty potato-bag.

Stumpy was unusually quiet. Audrey sensed he didn't know what to do with secrets either.

'The honeybag's in that tree.' Bloke lifted the billy can towards a tall tree with a straight trunk and thin leaves. She didn't have any fingers free to point. 'It's a blood-wood tree. Good for buildin'. Termites don't go for it so much. Wood's too hard.'

The beehive really *did* look like a bag.

Bees flew into a small opening in the trunk, then some flew out again.

'Did you track the bees with your bush eyes?' Audrey did a 'Dad' squint.

'I saw the wax on the trunk yesterday. Didn't have time before dark to collect the honey. Had no billy or axe with me either.'

'Those little bees aren't the stingy ones, are they?' asked Audrey.

'No. Native bees are friendly. The other sort, the big ones, *they* sting. Somebody brought them here from another country.'

'But if you came to a place that had friendly little bees with honeybags, why would you bring other ones that sting?'

'That's a good question, but I've got no answer. Thought I might have to chop into the trunk, but it's already split.' Reversing the axe, so that she was holding it by the head, Bloke poked the wooden handle into the nose of wax. 'Aborigines know how to find these honeybags, no trouble.'

Audrey felt her face go hot. It started at

her chin and worked up to her hairline. Her cubby wasn't too far from here and Bloke was a good walker.

'This woman once showed me how she got sticky stuff from some special leaves and glued a tiny cocky's feather onto the back of a bee,' added Bloke. 'Then she followed the bee to its honeybag. She could see the white feather real clear, and the feather slowed down the bee so she could keep up with it.'

Relief flooded through Audrey, and her legs shook. Bloke was only telling a story.

Striking quickly, Bloke poked the axe handle into the honeybag. More bees flew out. Audrey was glad the quandong seeds were dangling from her hat. She didn't want the bees bumping against her face, even if they didn't sting.

Honey ran down the tree trunk. Bloke dropped her axe and held the billy can against the trunk to catch it.

'Can I ask you something?' said Audrey.

'Sounds like you made up your mind to it already.'

Bloke kept her eyes on the honey.

That made it easier for Audrey to ask, 'Have you ever told a lie?'

'Why would you want to know that?'

Audrey shrugged. 'It just popped into my head. Ideas do that. They *jump* up by themselves.' Was that a fib? She didn't think so.

'My whole life was a lie,' said Bloke.

'That's an *awfully* big lie.' Audrey stuck her hand in the pocket of her trousers. Her fingers touched sticky jam, left over from Janet's bread. 'You don't have to tell me anything if you don't want. And sometimes people *can't* say things even when they want to.'

'Funny thing is, Two-Bob. I *do* want to tell you.' Bloke raised her right hand and licked honey from her forefinger. Then she went back to balancing the billy with both hands. 'Do people just look at you and start talkin'?'

'I might have to ask a question first.'

'I bet you might.' Bloke snorted. 'There's two kinds of people on the road. Them that are lookin' for something, goin' somewhere. And them that are runnin' away.'

Bloke stared out to the horizon. But she wasn't looking at the trees. Audrey guessed she was thinking about the city she'd left behind. And there was something there that she didn't like. Maybe Janet wasn't the only one running away.

Nineteen

Audrey's hand clenched around the top of the potato bag. A drumbeat of pulsing began in her ears.

She had seen something moving above the tops of the trees.

'I have to go ... oh, and Mum wants you to come for tea tonight,' Audrey told Bloke in a breathless string of words.

'But ...'

'Sorry. I just remembered I'm s'posed to be home by now.'

Audrey took off.

Her heart leapt as fast as her feet. She darted around trees and jumped over low bushes. There was no time to worry about treading on snakes or lizards. She had to get home, right away.

There was a line of cloud above the trees. For a split second Audrey thought it was smoke. But it wasn't the grey or black smoke of a bushfire. It was the deep red of dust.

Only a motor car or truck would make dust like that. Audrey had seen how dust billowed behind cars in Beltana.

Janet had said the men with too many buttons were in a car, and that they'd come looking for her. And now someone was driving away from Audrey's house!

She wished her feet would move faster.

The empty potato-bag caught on spiky spinifex. Audrey tugged, but it was snagged. She let go of the bag and ran on without it. There wasn't time to unhook it.

Stumpy pounded along behind her.

Her chest began to burn. A stitch nagged at her left side, under her ribs.

She didn't know whether to head home or go to the cubby.

But the dust was rising near the house. And if she ran towards Janet, she could accidentally show the men where Janet was hiding. They might see Audrey, or her footprints.

She curved towards the house.

Her family didn't know anything about Janet, so they wouldn't have to lie. Audrey was glad now that she'd kept the secret.

Dad wouldn't be scared by men who were dressed up like pet lizards. But if he argued with the policemen, they might put him in gaol.

Audrey tripped, but kept on her feet.

Home. She *had* to get home.

Twenty

Audrey shoved back the door and belted into the kitchen.

Mum sat at the table, cutting potatoes. She looked up, startled. 'What's the matter?' Her voice sounded breathless, as though she'd been the one running.

'Who was ... here?' Audrey's chest heaved as she tried to speak and breathe at the same time.

'The new mailman. In a truck.'

Audrey's legs trembled and she couldn't stop them. 'What did the mailman look like?'

Mum looked confused. 'He was of small build, with . . . unusual ears.'

'Why were his ears *unusual*?'

'Well, they were large.' Mum made a face, then she whispered, 'He looked like a mouse actually. His head was small and his face was wrinkled. Yet his ears were . . . flappy. I can't think of a more polite word. I think our new mailman was born with the wrong ears.'

'Did he have buttons?' Audrey ran one finger from her tummy up to her chin.

'I didn't notice. He wore braces over a shirt. So I suppose the shirt must have had buttons. But they didn't stand out.'

Audrey flumped onto a chair. Braces and a shirt were not how Janet described the policemen. They wore jackets with lots of buttons. The visitor had *not* been a buttoned policeman. Janet was safe—for now.

'What's so important about buttons?' asked Mum.

Audrey rested her elbows on the wooden

kitchen table. 'Buttons can tell you a lot about a person.'

'Is that so?' Her mum resumed cutting the potatoes into smaller pieces. Her knife clumped onto the wooden chopping board. It had the same regular beat as Dad's axe when he was splitting logs.

'Too many buttons could mean you're a show-off. And if you did *all* those buttons up, you'd have a face like this.' Audrey pushed her lips into a tight knot.

'If you have such a distaste for buttons, then perhaps I should stop calling you my "bright little button".'

Audrey smiled at her mum. 'But I'm only *one* button, so that's all right. And words sound different in your mouth because you love me.'

The kitchen door opened and Dad came in, with cabbages from the vegetable patch in his hands. His boots were powdered with red dust and his nails looked browner than usual.

'Do you want to know about buttons too?' Mum raised one eyebrow.

Dad looked suspiciously from Audrey to Mum. He half-closed his left eye as though that would make him see better. 'You two look like you're up to something.'

'It's all right, Dad,' said Audrey. 'Mum loves you too. Fair dinkum, she does. She always says you look nice in that shirt. Even though you wear it every day, even when you're all sweaty like a horse!' She grinned at him, happy that he was in the kitchen and not on his way to gaol.

Dad dumped the cabbages on the bench.

'Got animals to feed,' he muttered and retreated towards the kitchen door. He turned his head to wink at Audrey. 'I'll be back in time to change my shirt for dinner.'

'What's so important about buttons?' asked Mum.

Twenty-one

Douglas crawled from the sitting room into the kitchen. '*Broom, vrrrrrrr, vrrrr.*'

Audrey held out her arms.

Douglas scrambled onto her lap. He kicked her leg on the way up, but she didn't complain. He'd already forgotten about how upset he'd been earlier when she'd left him behind. She fluffed up his fringe. It was stuck to his forehead with sweat. Then she gave him a big hug.

'Dontsquashmeguts!' His little face went bright pink.

'What was that?' Mum put down the knife and wiped her hands on her green apron.

'He said not to hug him so tight.' Audrey didn't include the word 'guts'. Her mum had strong ideas about which words were not suitable for children.

Douglas wriggled free and slipped to the floor. He got back down on his hands and knees and resumed being a car. Although, since the mailman had come in a truck, Douglas was probably being a truck. Which was like a car, but noisier.

Mum stood up and fetched the earthenware jug from the side bench. She brought it to the table, took off the lace doily which kept out bugs and poured water into a glass. 'Here. Your face is as red as a beetroot.'

Audrey picked up the glass and drank till it was empty. She felt the water sloshing down into her tummy. Audrey wiped the back of her hand across her top lip. 'I ran really fast when I saw the dust. Bet the new mailman didn't say *peanuts* like Mr Akbar.'

'No, he didn't.' Mum refilled Audrey's glass. 'Drink a little slower this time. If you keep going at that rate, you could drown.'

Audrey sipped at the second glass.

'There are two letters for you. One from Jimmy and the other from Mrs Paterson. I put them on your bed.'

Letters didn't come that often. Usually, Audrey could hardly wait to tear open the envelopes and read them. Today, she had more urgent things on her mind.

'I told Bloke to come for tea,' said Audrey, to remind Mum that she'd been on an errand for her.

Mum took the water jug back to the bench. 'You and Bloke must've had an exciting time. You've been gone for quite a while ...'

'Me and Bloke found a honeybag and we were discussening life and things.'

'That would explain how long it took you. Life is a pretty big topic to discuss.'

Mum rubbed her round tummy with one hand. With the apron tied around her waist, her stomach looked even bigger. Audrey wondered if the baby could hear her voice. Mum pulled out the chair next to Audrey and sank into it with a grunt.

'Is the baby getting heavy?'

'It certainly is. I've only got one good leg and it's carrying around two of us.'

Douglas *vroomed* his way around the kitchen table. He knocked into the meat safe and it wobbled. Water splashed onto the mud floor.

'Careful, Dougie,' said Mum, without taking her eyes off Audrey.

'Bloke and me were talking about . . . lies. What *is* a lie, really?

'Audrey, do you ever think of *small* questions that have simple answers?'

'Every question is big if you don't have an answer. It won't go away until you know.'

A tiny smile started on Mum's lips. 'A lie is when you say something that isn't true.'

'If you believe something, does that make it true?' Audrey sipped at her water like a bird. She felt like gulping. But her mum was paying close attention and she expected sips.

'No, it doesn't make it *true*. But we can only do and say what we think is right. We *try*. So when we put our heads down on our pillows at night, we feel we did our best for that day, and we sleep soundly.'

'I believe in Stumpy, but some people don't.'

'Audrey, you listen with your heart. Some people can't do that. And they don't want to. Listening with your heart makes everything loud and, sometimes, difficult.' Mum took Audrey's fingers in hers. 'Oh, but the things you see ... *wonderful* things.'

Audrey let go of Mum's hand and picked up the glass in both hands. 'If a troll was after me, would you lie so it couldn't find me?'

'I'd rather *not* lie,' said Mum. 'But I suppose if I *had* to, to save you from a troll, then I would. Trolls, I'm told, are quite mean. But if I *did* lie, you'd look at me differently after that.'

'I would?'

'You'd be looking at someone who'd lied. Maybe you wouldn't quite trust me any more.'

'But you saved me from getting gobbled by a troll!'

'Yes, and that would be worth giving something up.' Mum sighed. She had tired lines around her eyes. Her cheeks were two bright red patches. 'Of course, I could only help if you *told* me about the troll. Couldn't I?'

Audrey plonked the glass on the table. 'Lucky trolls aren't real.'

Twenty-two

The sun slipped below the horizon. Audrey watched as the brilliant red, and then the gold, began to fade. Sunset colours changed quickly. If you looked away for a few seconds, then back again, they were different. Audrey's favourite was the deep blue that came just after the crimson and gold faded and the first star came out. She wondered if Janet was watching for that star too.

'It's your turn.'

Audrey jumped at the sound of Bloke's voice.

She sat cross-legged in front of Audrey, looking like a mountain with a head. 'We're startin' again with Ones, in case you forgot.'

Tapping her chin with her forefinger, Audrey stared at the five sheep knucklebones on the ground.

Nearby, the goats bleated in their pen, and the chooks made soft clucking noises. Once the sun went down, the chooks went to roost. Nimrod hardly seemed to sleep at all. A dog or fox would have to be especially brave to challenge *him*.

Audrey picked up the knucklebones, but looked up at the sky again. There it was, the first star! Her fingers squeezed the knucklebones firmly into her right palm. *Star light, star bright; I wish I may, I wish I might, have the wish I wish tonight* ... She imagined Janet running to her mother, then sent her wish flying all the way up to the big, twinkling star.

'You got something on your mind?' asked Bloke.

'*Lots* of things. Do you reckon people's heads are ever quiet?'

'Depends on the person. If I get to worryin' then I take off, go somewhere new. Walkin' makes me so tired I can't worry no more.'

Audrey threw the five knucklebones in the air and turned her hand over. One knuckle fell on the back of her hand. Four landed on the ground.

'Sometimes talkin' to someone helps,' said Bloke.

Audrey kept her eyes on the knuckle-bones. She had a funny feeling at the back of her neck, like a tickle. Bloke's voice sounded different, softer.

Her hand moving quickly, Audrey threw a knucklebone in the air, scooped another from the ground and opened her hand again to catch the first in midair.

'Gettin' hard to see,' said Bloke. 'Light'll be gone soon.'

It *was* growing darker and the air was

nippy. Audrey could hear the rattle of cutlery from inside the house. Then Douglas bellowed a flurry of words. The smell of roast meat made Audrey's mouth water.

Bloke took a deep breath. 'I used to play knucklebones in the orphanage.'

'But Price said your parents were loggers and you lived in camps.'

'That was when I was real little. But then my mother got sick with her lungs,' said Bloke. 'The old man sent me and my three brothers to an orphanage. Don't reckon he liked children. He was always complainin' we made too much noise. He didn't like play, my dad. If you weren't workin' you was wastin' time.'

Audrey peered at Bloke. Sometimes faces showed feelings that words did not. But the dimming light made Bloke's face hard to read.

'Me and my brother Melvin used to hop the fence and look in the rubbish bins at the school next door cos we was always hungry,' said Bloke. 'That's probably why I'm the size of a shed. If there's food, I eat it. Just in case there won't be none the next day. Got sick of being hungry . . . and other things. So I lit outa there. Jumped a train, came out bush.'

'All by yourself?'

'At first. I was living rough. Then Maud and Thomas found me.'

'Did they adoptinate you?'

'Sorta. It was lucky they found me. I was young, see. And scared.'

Audrey couldn't imagine Bloke being scared of anything.

'I haven't seen my brothers in twenty years, that's the noise I've got in *my* head.'

Twenty years was a long time. Janet might end up separated from *her* family for that long, maybe forever, if she didn't get home.

'We all need someone to help us, some-time or other . . .' Bloke didn't ask a question, yet her words seemed like one.

Audrey rubbed at her arms to smooth out

the goosebumps, then scooped up the knucklebones. It was too dark to continue the game and she wanted to go inside.

'What's the noise in *your* head, Audrey?' asked Bloke.

'Come and get it,' Mum called through the open window.

Audrey jumped up at the sound of her mum's voice and held out her hand to Bloke. 'We have to go in now. Mum's been cooking for hours.'

Bloke uncurled her legs, groaned, and took Audrey's hand to steady herself. There were calluses along the base of Bloke's fingers. Hard little nuts of skin that proved she'd swung her axe many times.

Audrey was glad that Bloke had told her about her family. But she couldn't confide in her in return. The noise in Audrey's head—the secret about Janet—had gone from whispers to shouts. But she couldn't share them. Not with anyone.

Twenty-three

Audrey pushed her large treasure-tin back under her bed. It had once contained biscuits. But now it held Audrey's special things. And until tomorrow morning, it would also hold a lump of roasted kangaroo that she'd sneaked out of the kitchen for Janet. It wasn't exactly 'treasure'. Except if you were hungry. And by the time Audrey could sneak to the cubby tomorrow, Janet would be exactly that.

The meat had a strong smell. But Audrey hoped no one would detect it now that it was snugly in the tin with the lid shut. Otherwise, her mum and dad would want to know why she was hiding food. It would be hard to explain without giving away the secret about Janet.

There was a thump on the roof over Audrey's head, then a scrabbling of little feet. Hot pins and needles ran down her arms. It was only another possum on the roof. They often jumped about up there. But the sudden sound had startled her.

Keeping this secret was like wearing a prickly shirt. No matter how much you wriggled and scratched, it would still be uncomfortable.

There was a lot of noise coming from the kitchen. Bloke's voice boomed. And everyone else was louder because of it.

Audrey wished she could go to Janet right now, but she knew she'd be missed. So instead, she picked up her letter from Jimmy and carried it through the sitting room to the kitchen.

'I could have sworn there was half a rabbit left in here,' said Mum, as she looked in the meat safe.

Audrey stopped suddenly in the doorway. The cooked rabbit had only been a scrawny little leftover. She'd hoped no one would notice it was gone.

She shot a look around the room.

Douglas sat on Dad's lap, his thumb in his mouth. His eyelids drooped.

Price was stacking dishes on the shelves.

Bloke scrubbed at the roasting dish with a brush. On summer nights, dishes were washed outside. Now, it was too cold at night and washing up was done in a large metal basin on the bench.

'Price, did you take that rabbit?' asked Mum.

'No!' He sent her a look that said, *Why would I want half a skinny rabbit?*

'Never mind, Everhilda.' said Dad. 'Sit down now. That's enough work for one day.'

'I was going to give that meat to Bloke in exchange for the honey.'

'Don't you worry about that, Mrs B,' said Bloke. 'If I ate any more I'd burst. You're a bonzer cook.'

Audrey's mouth felt dry. She called out to distract everyone from the missing meat. 'Want to hear what's in Jimmy's letter?'

All eyes turned her way.

Twenty-four

Dad wrapped his arms around Douglas and stood up. 'Give us two secs.'

Audrey moved back to let Dad through. She didn't look at him in case he guessed *she'd* taken the meat.

'Dontwannagotobed,' protested Douglas.

But he was quiet after that.

The others trooped into the sitting room.

Audrey's mum picked up her sewing. 'Would you like to sit here, Bloke? Beside me.'

'I'm right, thanks, Mrs B. I'll head back to camp soon. Might just hear the news first.'

Bloke shuffled from one foot to the other. Her huge body made the sitting room seem smaller.

Dad came back and turned up the lamps on the side table and mantelpiece. Ignoring his tattered but comfortable armchair, he sat beside Mum on the sofa and fingered the shirt she was taking in for Price. 'That was a good shirt. Had it for years.'

'It might have been good once,' said Mum in the voice she used when she was being teacher in the mornings. 'But it's seen better days.'

'Did I look like a sweaty horse in it?' Dad grinned wickedly.

Mum lightly smacked his hand.

'What's in your letter, Mum?' asked Audrey. She wondered if her voice sounded squeaky.

Price sat in Dad's armchair and stretched out his legs.

Audrey decided against the rug where she usually sat in the evening. Instead, she moved to stand next to Bloke, with her back against the wall.

'I had a letter from Mrs Paterson,' said Mum, with a smile. 'She's offered to come and help when I have the baby.'

'Mrs Paterson's not as bad as she looks, is she? She's got a bigger good side than anyone thought,' said Audrey quickly, glad Mum seemed to have forgotten about the missing rabbit meat.

Then there was a silence that Audrey immediately tried to fill. 'Price, what's in *your* letter from Jimmy?'

He slipped down in the armchair. 'Some bloke called Mawson went to the Antarctic.'

'Is that near Adelaide?'

Wood crackled on the fire, hissing sparks.

'See what happens when you skip out on lessons, Audrey?' Mum paused, with the needle and cotton firmly between her finger and thumb. 'The Antarctic is a long way south of Adelaide. Right at the bottom of the world.'

A gust of wind blew down the chimney and the fire burned more strongly. Wind was nature's bellows, Dad sometimes said.

'Mrs Paterson says in her letter that she wants to give me something,' said Audrey. 'It has four legs and barks.' Normally she would've been more excited, but tonight her mind was on other things.

'A new dog! Can we, Dad?' Price sat up straight in his chair. He suddenly looked like a boy again.

'Don't see why not.'

'And Jimmy sent me a picture from the newspaper.' Audrey handed it to Bloke first. 'This lady's called Amy Johnson and she flyded a plane from Britain to Australia. All by herself. It took *nineteen* days.'

'Now that *is* remarkable.' Mum smiled. 'But I believe the word is *flew*.'

'She *flewed* the plane.' Audrey looked again at the newspaper cutting in Bloke's hands. Amy Johnson had shiny eyes and a determined mouth. Her eyebrows were long and thin, like someone had drawn them on her face with a pencil. Her fur collar went right up around her face. And she wore a tight cap with goggles on top. If Janet could fly a plane she could get home quick smart.

'Listen!' said Price.

Audrey held her breath. Was it a car?

No. It was rain on the roof. Gentle and steady.

Dad's nose hadn't smelled *this* rain. Or, if it did, he hadn't let on.

Audrey worried again about Janet out in the cubby. It was solid, but the roof wouldn't keep out *all* the rain. Janet would be wearing the red cardigan, and huddling under the thin old blanket. Cold water would be dripping on her. She could get sick. Then Audrey would have to tell her parents about Janet and why she was hiding.

But if Audrey did that, she'd be breaking her promise to Janet. She hadn't spat on her hand and promised to get warts. Janet hadn't asked her to do that. But breaking a promise was like lying. And Audrey didn't want to imagine what her parents would say if they found out that she'd let Janet hide in her cubby and sneaked her food from the kitchen. Janet might not be the only one to get into trouble.

Janet limped up and down.

Twenty-five

Audrey looked back at her footprints and frowned. Last night's rain had washed away traces of her old footprints. But it had made softer soil for new ones.

There were other marks in the ground. One footprint and one small hole; then another footprint and small hole. Audrey smiled to herself. She knew just what had caused those marks.

She came around a thick cluster of trees and saw Janet standing by the cubbyhouse, with a thin branch propped under one arm.

She wore Audrey's red cardigan over her own fawn one. It was too big for her so she'd folded back the sleeves.

'G'day,' called Audrey.

'I been waitin' to show you ... look!' Janet limped up and down, as though she was a guard on sentry duty in front of the cubbyhouse. But it was a big limp. She was almost hopping, and her mouth was tight. Each step was obviously painful.

'You're *walking*, said Audrey.

'I been practising.'

'And you look pretty in the red cardigan. But can we sit down now? I walked real fast.' Audrey figured that Janet would sit if *she* did. 'And cop this!' She held up the lump of roasted kangaroo meat.

'You gonna wipe your feet away?'

Audrey glanced down at her laced boots. 'They're joined onto my legs.'

'Your feet. In the ground.'

'Oh, you mean my *footprints*.'

'That's what I said. Get some of that

brush over there. Wipe your feet back to that rock. We're done walking for now, so we should take those prints away.'

Audrey hadn't thought of doing that. She handed over the kangaroo meat. Then she grabbed a piece of broken brush and swept it, left and right, across the ground. The footprints disappeared.

Behind her, Audrey heard Janet, hopping and *ouch*ing into the cubby. Then there was a loud grunt. She guessed that was Janet lowering herself to the ground.

Backing up to the cubby, Audrey made sure all traces of their footsteps were gone. Then she lifted the brush door into place.

'Some people, if they're sneakin', they walk backwards. Looks like they goin' the other way. But tracker would still find them.'

'Why did you want me to sweep away our footprints then?' Audrey crossed her legs.

Janet looked at Audrey from under half-closed lids. 'Not everyone's a tracker.' She lifted the kangaroo meat and began to nibble at it.

Audrey looked down at the notebook and pencils. The book lay open on the ground.

'Oh, you drew a picture.' Audrey pointed to the book. 'It looks nice.'

Janet paused between bites. 'I drew a *story*. About me and you. See?'

Audrey picked up the notebook. The patterns on the page were pretty. There were circles and lines, grouped around a larger ring in the centre of the page. 'This line of marks here, that looks like footprints.'

Janet kept chewing, but nodded.

There was a second line of markings. A footprint then a dot, a footprint and dot. 'That's you! Your foot and the stick.'

Janet looked pleased.

'Um. This one with all the little lines, that has to be rain.'

The pictures *were* telling a story.

'I know this one. Bet that's emu foot-prints. Seen *them* lots of times.' Audrey studied the page seeking more clues. 'Is that one a bush?'

'Those bushes out there.'

'What are these little circles?'

'Ants.'

'Plenty of them around here. More than you could shake a stick at. And this one.' Audrey did a 'Dad' squint. 'What's that?'

'Possum feet. He runnin' all over the top last night. Noisy fella.'

'*We* had a possum on our roof last night.'

Janet rested the remaining meat on her left knee. She rubbed her hands together. 'You sure that was just possum?'

'Sounded like a possum to me.'

Janet leaned forward to whisper, 'Spirit, maybe.'

'Why would a spirit play on the roof?'

Janet looked around as though she expected a ghostly figure to pop up beside them in the cubby. 'They do what they want, spirits. Who gonna tell 'em not to go up there?'

Audrey nodded, then flipped through more pages in the notebook. Janet had sketched as though she was lying on a cloud, looking down. The symbols were flat, like patterns. *Familiar* patterns.

'This here ...' Audrey traced a path with her forefinger. 'This is a square like our house. And that could be the tank stand. That one's like the dunny.' She looked up.

Grease glistened on Janet's chin.

'This *is* my house!' cried Audrey. 'How do you know what it looks like?'

'Been there. I seen something. A big light and it moved out the back of your place.'

Shivers ran down Audrey's spine. 'I saw something too. And it was out the back. It was sort of pale and it moved above the ground. If you saw it too, then it *is* real.'

She couldn't wait to tell Price.

Then she remembered that she couldn't tell him anything about it. Janet was a secret.

'But ...' Audrey rubbed at her forehead.

'You can't walk. When did you see my house?'

'Night of the big dust storm.'

'That's the night *I* saw the ghost! If we both saw it at the same time, then ...' Audrey stopped. She looked at Janet's smock. At night, her legs wouldn't show up, but the pale smock-dress would.

'*You're* the ghost.'

'No!' Janet shook her head. 'I'm a girl.'

'I mean, I reckon I saw *you*.'

'You saw me?'

'And you saw *me*.'

'I only seen you here.'

'I went out to the dunny on the night of the dust storm,' explained Audrey. 'And I was holding up a hurricane lamp. That was the light! You couldn't see me properly, cos of the dust.'

Janet gave a sheepish grin. 'You and me, we gonna be friends till our teeth fall out. Even our spirits know each other.'

Audrey smiled at Janet, but it quickly

faded. 'I might not see you again after you go. I don't know where you live.'

Janet blinked her thick eyelashes. 'I know *your* place. One day, I'll come back. First, I have to get out of here and go home.' Leaning forward, Janet ran her fingers gently over her swollen ankle. 'This gonna make me slow walkin'.'

'You'll get hungry.'

'All the time, hungry.'

'Me too,' said Audrey. 'You'll need a bag to carry food. Mum's got lots of hessian bags. I can get another one and start putting food in there so you can carry it.'

'And water. I get thirsty when I'm walkin'.'

Just *talking* about doing something made Audrey feel better, and Janet looked more cheerful.

But even while they were talking, the police and a tracker were probably searching for Janet. If Janet's ankle didn't heal soon, the men would find her.

Twenty-six

Audrey dropped her pencil and flexed her fingers.

Mum looked up from her sewing.

'I've got prickles in my fingers,' said Audrey. 'I'm just stretching them.'

'That's all right, dear. Your arithmetic will still be waiting when you're finished.'

Audrey sighed.

Douglas, playing trains with a small tin on the floor, hiccupped. Then he giggled.

'Is a hiccup when your teeth are coughing, Everhilda?' said Audrey.

Price snorted and then pretended that he was coughing instead of laughing.

Mum looked across the table at Audrey. Her expression was both mother *and* teacher. 'When we're having lessons, it would be better not to use my first name, dear.' Her eyes twinkled. 'I seem to remember a certain young lady wanting to be called Miss Barlow when she tried being teacher.'

'But that didn't work.' Audrey rubbed her hands together. 'Price was naughty.'

Her brother's head shot up. 'I *was* not.' The end of Price's pencil was chewed. When he was stuck for answers, he nibbled it.

Douglas hiccupped again.

'Audrey, you're not going outside till it's finished,' said Mum. 'The longer you delay and cause distractions, the longer it will take you.'

'Bloke saw snow when she went to Victoria,' said Audrey. 'What *is* snow?'

'We're doing numbers today.'

'I can't think about numbers cos there's

no room in my head. It keeps wondering about snow. Is snow when clouds shiver?'

'Well, just pretend the numbers are snowflakes. Then you can add them up.'

Audrey sighed, but gave in and tried to make sense of the numbers on her page. But then she looked up, startled. 'What's that noise?'

'*Audrey!*' Mum's eyes widened in warning.

'Hang on, I can hear something too,' said Price.

Audrey felt a chill that had nothing to do with snow *or* arithmetic and everything to do with being afraid. She felt frozen in her chair, unable to move, not even to stand up and check what was coming towards the house.

Mum, Price and Audrey turned their heads towards the back of the house. Even Douglas stopped his tin 'train' to listen.

Audrey looked towards the window where Stumpy usually stood during lessons. He often stuck his camel head between the curtains and pulled faces to make Audrey giggle. But today, Stumpy wasn't there. Maybe he was watching over Janet out at the cubby.

'Is that the mailman back again?' Mum frowned. 'He's not due for two months.'

Price jumped up, rushed to the door and flung it open.

The goats were bleating their heads off, and Nimrod, the big rooster, crowed to show how tough he was.

The sound of a motor became louder.

'It's a car!' shouted Price.

Audrey's heart leapt. Her chest hurt.

A big black car, covered in red dust, pulled to a stop.

The driver's door opened.

A man got out.

He wore a peaked hat that shaded his eyes. His shoes were unusually shiny. And his dark jacket had a long row of equally shiny buttons.

Twenty-seven

The policeman sat his cup back in the saucer. 'That was delicious, Mrs Barlow.'

Audrey's mum smiled, but it didn't reach her eyes. She stood with her back to the bench. Usually when there were visitors, she sat with them at the table.

'More tea?' asked Mum.

'I won't say no. Thank you. It's camel country out here, a long time between drinks.' He laughed heartily. His teeth were yellow and higgledy-piggledy although the rest of him was neat, tidy and buttoned.

Mum stepped to the table and picked up the teapot. Her cheeks were red even though the kitchen was cool. She poured strong, brown tea into the policeman's cup. Her eyes fixed on his jacket buttons, then she raised them to look across at Audrey. Their eyes held. Then Audrey looked aside.

Audrey thought hard. What could she do to warn Janet? Make an excuse to go to her room, then climb out the window and run to the cubby? No, that would look suspicious. The policeman could easily follow her and, with a car, he'd catch up to her in no time at all. He was here in the kitchen, so that meant he hadn't found Janet yet. But he was close. *Too* close.

Through the open kitchen door, Audrey saw Price run his hand along the car's bonnet. His fingers left streaks in the dust.

'Don't touch the vehicle, young fellow,' called the policeman. 'We can't have any damage. Government property, you know.'

Price snatched back his hand.

Audrey glanced out at the Aboriginal man, who had come with the policeman. The man stood by the car. His wide-brimmed hat was pushed back on his head. He had a small beard that was cut close to his face. He'd rolled up the sleeves of his fawn shirt as far as his elbows. He didn't have shiny shoes, like the policeman. Instead, he wore pull-on boots that were as dusty as the car. The buckle on his trouser belt was shiny though, and so were his eyes. They looked everywhere, but he hadn't spoken a word.

Audrey swallowed over a lump in her throat. Her mouth was dry, but she didn't want to draw attention to herself by asking for a drink.

'Would your ... would the other gentleman like some tea?' asked Mum.

'Oh. The tracker?' said the policeman. 'Your boy can give him some water outside.'

Mum's mouth tightened into a straight line. She turned to take another cup from the shelf and filled it with tea from the pot.

'Audrey, dear, would you take this to the gentleman outside?'

The policeman gave Mum a look that hinted that he wasn't happy that she'd ignored him.

Audrey looked down as she picked up the cup. From the corner of her eye, she saw the policeman dig out two large spoons of sugar from the bowl for his tea, stir it, then tap his spoon on the cup. He slurped, and then clicked the cup back onto the saucer.

'Are you *sure* you haven't seen the girl, Mrs Barlow?' the policeman asked.

Audrey's mum shook her head. 'I haven't been far from the house lately.'

The policeman stared at Mum's round tummy. Audrey wanted to tell him not to, but she didn't dare. That tummy belonged to the family. The baby was theirs. He wasn't allowed to look.

Mum's face went even redder. 'My husband will be home soon.'

'What about you, child?'

Audrey froze.

He was looking at *her*. Talking to her.

But she couldn't look at *him*. Her tongue seemed stuck to the roof of her mouth.

'My daughter has been helping me quite a lot lately,' said Mum. 'Extra chores. My leg isn't too good, you see. A tank stand fell on it some years ago and crushed it.'

Audrey had never heard her mum say so many private words to a stranger. Mum seldom talked about the accident or whether her leg was painful.

'Go on, dear. Take out that cup of tea before it goes cold.' Mum sounded breathless.

Douglas had lost interest in the visitors already. He'd gone back to playing trains on the dry mud floor. Audrey stepped around him, the cup held carefully in both hands. She felt prickly with perspiration.

'We don't see many visitors,' said Mum. 'The children are shy.'

Audrey stepped outside.

'This lost Aboriginal girl, she's out there all alone. Anything could happen to her,' said the policeman. 'We're taking her to a place where she'll be looked after and she'll learn to be useful. She needs discipline. It's the best thing for her.' He wiped tea from his mouth with one finger. 'Perhaps the girl's been around here and you haven't realised. Have you had any food go missing, or clothes?'

Mum cleared her throat.

Audrey had her back to her mum, and she didn't dare turn around. Her feet kept moving towards the man in the broad-brimmed hat by the car. If Mum told the policeman about the rabbit meat, he'd know Janet was nearby. He'd discover that Audrey had given food to Janet. Audrey didn't know if they put little girls in gaol. They might. Janet had been in a place where they wouldn't let her go home. Audrey figured they'd put *her* there too.

'I think I'd notice if food went missing.'

Mum gave a tight laugh. It wasn't her real laugh, but a stranger might think she was amused. 'With five of us here and another on the way, we need every scrap we can find.'

Audrey approached the Aboriginal man and held out the cup.

She flicked a look at him, just for a second.

His right eye twitched.

Did it always do that, or had he just winked at her? Audrey didn't dare look up at him again. He might see in her eyes that she was hiding something.

Janet had said a good tracker could find *anyone, anywhere*. He could tell everything but what they ate for lunch. And maybe even that. This tracker was already so close to where Janet was hiding. He'd find her, and then they'd take her away in the big black car. Her mum and aunties would be calling her and she might *never* answer.

Twenty-eight

The car drove off, back the way it came. For now, it was heading away from Janet.

If she saw the car, she'd be scared. She might try to hop away, but she wouldn't get far. Or would she huddle inside the cubby and hope the policeman and tracker didn't see her? Whatever happened, she was out there alone.

Audrey, Price and Mum stood outside the house, watching the dust cloud. Douglas was inside, still playing trains. He was the only one who didn't feel the tightness in the air. It was just as though a thunderstorm was brewing, when the air was charged, ready to spark. But there were no clouds in the sky. The thunderstorm was right there on the ground.

Mum took Audrey's hand.

Audrey squeezed her fingers.

'You took that meat, didn't you, Sis?' said Price.

Audrey nodded.

'Where is she?' Mum's fingers twitched against Audrey's.

It was a direct question. One that Audrey could not avoid answering. Besides, Mum already knew she'd seen 'the girl'. Even if they hadn't spoken the words to each other. And Audrey couldn't lie straight out to Mum.

'In my pirate cubby.'

Mum's cheeks were still red, but there were white patches beneath her eyes.

'What are we going to do?' said Audrey. 'They'll send her to some place where she has to wash floors and carry big buckets. And it's too hard for a little girl.'

'I'm not sure we can do anything.' Mum sighed. 'It's the law. That was a policeman. I don't know what your father's going to say about this. We should have told the police what we know. And we can't actually *stop* them.'

'You did good, Mum.' Audrey squeezed her hand yet again. 'Janet said her family are calling for her *every* day. She wants to go home to her mum. If a policeman came to take *me* away, Janet would try to stop them. She's little, but she's strong. Except for her bung foot. She can't walk properly.'

Mum bit her lip.

'I have to warn her,' said Audrey. '*Please* don't tell me not to go.' Her legs jiggled. Her feet wanted to run.

Her mum said nothing.

Audrey slipped her hand free of her mother's warm grasp and swallowed hard.

'If I go to gaol, you can have my treasure

tin,' she told Price. 'There's a ripper emu egg in there. You can put it on your string.'

Price rolled his eyes. 'I don't want your egg. You keep it. You won't go to gaol. Besides, I'm coming with you.'

Every second counted.

Twenty-nine

Audrey ran. Usually Price was faster because his legs were longer. But this time he matched his pace to hers.

'What are we going to do when we find the girl?' asked Price, his words short and clipped from lack of air.

'Janet,' said Audrey. 'Her name's *Janet*. And I'll take her home to our house.'

'Audrey, she isn't a kitten you can drag around with you.'

She swerved around a thick cluster of trees, dodged a tall ant hill and kept running.

Her feet hit the ground as she belted along and she felt it all the way up to her knees. Both of her thick plaits bounced against her back.

'Dad'll be back soon. Then we can work out what to do.' She slowed again and pointed to a slab of rock. 'This way. We won't leave footprints if we run on hard rock.'

Price looked at her. He seemed surprised that she'd had such a clever idea.

There wasn't time to stop and try to brush away their footsteps. Every second counted.

'Wish we had the billycart,' she called to her brother. 'We could tow Janet home.'

The billycart had been left out in the bush somewhere and there had been no time to search for it. Douglas often dragged it behind him into the bushes, but returned without it. It was like hide-and-seek, but without the seek.

'It'd be slow going in the sand,' said Price. 'I'll piggyback her if she can't walk.'

That would work. Janet was only small and she wouldn't weigh much.

'Let's go that way.' Audrey pointed to their left.

Price and Audrey leapt from one sheet of flat rock to another, until the rock petered out.

Then they were back on red sandy soil. The sound of their running feet changed in the soft sand.

Audrey stumbled. Her legs were tired.

Price grabbed her arm, but she stayed on her feet. Her cubbyhouse had never seemed so far away. She wondered if people could run so far and so fast that they melted into a heap on the ground.

Finally she saw her cubby through the trees. 'There it is,' she panted.

Price didn't answer. He was puffing hard.

Audrey forgot about her sore feet and the painful heat in her chest. All she could think about was reaching the cubby and getting Janet back to the house.

Price shot ahead. He crashed right through a large saltbush instead of running around it.

He stopped abruptly, his chest heaving.

Audrey was only seconds behind him. She caught up, ignoring the stitch in her left side.

She looked down at the ground. There were no footprints. No sign that anyone had been here.

'Wait here,' Audrey whispered to Price. 'She'll be scared of you.'

Audrey crept forward and whistled.

There was no answer.

'Janet,' she hissed.

The only sound she heard was the wind in the bushes. Then the crows: *caa, caa, caa.*

Audrey pulled the brush door aside.

Thirty

Price poked his head inside the cubbyhouse. 'Are you all right, Audrey?'

Audrey looked up at him. The sun was bright behind him and his body looked dark and tall, like a shadow.

'She's not here.'

Audrey's red cardigan had been dropped on the ground inside the cubby. The notebook, pencils scattered around it, was next to the cardigan.

Price squatted on his heels in the open doorway. 'They must've got her.' His voice was hushed, as though he was nervous about waking someone from sleep.

Audrey's heart was thumping around in her chest and she couldn't think properly. She'd tried to protect Janet. But the men had caught her anyway. Audrey couldn't speak straight away. If she did, she'd start crying.

Janet would be scared, and upset that she couldn't reach her mum and her aunties. She might even be angry. But it wouldn't make any difference how she felt. Those men with the buttons would still take her down to Quorn to carry heavy buckets and iron clothes.

'She . . .' Audrey swallowed. 'Janet's only little. A strong wind would blow her over. What's her mum going to do when she doesn't come home?'

Price reached one hand out towards Audrey, then let it drop. 'I'm sorry, Sis.' He cleared his throat. 'Why'd they leave this stuff behind?'

'I don't . . .' Audrey paused, tapping her chin with one finger. Then she said, 'There's no prints.'

'What?'

'There's no footprints, no marks on the ground. If those men dragged Janet out to the car, there'd be marks in the sand. They wouldn't come back to wipe out their footprints.'

'Has she walked out by herself?' asked Price. 'I thought you said she couldn't walk properly.'

'She can't. Her ankle looks like a paddy-melon. It's all puffy.'

Audrey picked up the notebook and opened it.

'I don't understand,' said Price. 'Did she leave you a note?'

Audrey studied the open pages of the notebook before answering, 'Sort of.'

She turned the book around to show Price what Janet had drawn on the page. The pictures looked as though they'd been done in a hurry, and weren't nearly as neat as Janet's usual drawings.

'Why are you showing me pictures?'

'They're not just *pictures*. They're *stories*.'

She beckoned her brother inside the cubby. Price had to bend over to fit under the roof.

'Look!' said Audrey. 'This circle is the cubby. That line means she's left the cubby and she's travelling somewhere. I don't know where. I can't read it good enough. See these shapes, the small one and the bigger one?'

Price nodded.

Audrey moved her finger across the page. 'The small one's Janet and the other, big one, is a grown-up. She's gone *with* someone.'

'But who? The policeman?'

Audrey shook her head. 'See this shape, like a little bag? It's where the native bees keep their honey.'

Price looked puzzled.

'Bloke found the honeybag.' Audrey closed her eyes and held the book to her chest.

'What's Bloke got to do with Janet?'

'Janet is telling me that Bloke has taken her, without saying it's her!' said Audrey. 'She's smart, Janet.'

'Are you sure Bloke's got her?'

'Too right. They were running away on their own. Now they're running away *together*.'

'Will Janet get home to her mum?' asked Audrey.

Thirty-one

Audrey knelt on the ground beside the wooden crosses at the back of her house. She held red and brown wildflowers together while her mum tied a bow around each bunch.

Then her mum placed one bunch on Esther's grave, and the other on Pearl's.

'Will Janet get home to her mum?' asked Audrey.

'I hope so. She sounds a determined little girl. And Bloke's strong, she'll be able to carry a little girl like that, no problems, even with her swag. Bloke's been on the road for years and she knows the bush well. I'm sure she'll do her best to take Janet back to her mother.'

'Bloke was in a place that made her sad when she was little, just like Janet. Then she met a new mum and dad. Bloke's got three brothers and she hasn't seen them for a long time. I reckon Janet and Bloke are both girls looking for their families. 'Cept Bloke's a lot older and she's got no teeth.'

'When did Bloke meet Janet?'

'They didn't tell me. But I think Bloke might have known about Janet before Janet knew about *her*. Bloke was sort of ... *different* when we were playing knuckle-bones. It was like I had an itch on my back, but I didn't know exactly where to scratch it. Bloke was trying to say something and I didn't get it.' Audrey lowered her voice to a whisper. 'I reckon secrets make people different. Anyway, I thought she was talking about *her* family.'

Mum patted Audrey's hand.

'Will I ever see Janet again?'

'One day, maybe.'

'Dad said he'd tell me more about Pearl and Esther *one day*. But he hasn't done it yet.'

Mum brushed twigs from the ground around the bunches of flowers. 'He will, when he's ready.'

'*You* could tell me all about them instead.'

'I think your father wants to do it. Be patient with him. He's working up to it. He took two years to get the courage to ask my father if he could marry me.'

'Was your dad a dogger, like Dad?'

'No, he was a camel breeder.'

In a nearby tree top, a kookaburra laughed.

Audrey turned to look at the tethered camels. Stumpy stood with them. He wasn't tied, but sometimes he liked to talk to other camels. Audrey heard Janet's voice in her head, *That camel, he your family?*

A shiver ran down Audrey's spine.

Janet was the biggest secret Audrey had ever had. The secret was almost *too* big. Bloke also had a secret, about the orphanage and her lost brothers. Audrey wondered if *everybody* had secrets.

'Mum . . . have you ever lied to me?'

'If I say *no*, straight out, that could be a lie. But I try *not* to lie.'

'Do you tell me *everything*?' asked Audrey.

'Not everything. Some thoughts in my mind are grown-up things.'

'You knew I had a secret, didn't you, Mum?'

'I suspected.'

Audrey reached out and helped Mum brush twigs and pebbles from the girls' graves. 'When mums sus-pec-t, that means they *know*. You didn't *ask* me about my secret.'

'I was waiting for you to decide what to do,' said Mum.

'What if I decided wrong?'

'If I made every choice for you, you

wouldn't learn to make your own. And I trusted you to make the right one in the end. The hardest choices are not between right and wrong, but between two rights . . . *ooh.*' Mum put one hand on her swollen tummy.

'Are you all right?' Audrey leaned closer to her mum.

'It's the baby. He just decided to play football.' Mum took Audrey's hand and held it against her tummy.

Something small and firm pushed against Audrey's hand. 'I can feel it,' she whispered. 'But girls can play footie, too. It might be a girl.'

'Audrey Barlow, you are quite right.'

'There's been a lot of secrets around here lately, but I know one thing that's *not* a secret. This is the best family in the whole, right to the edge, across the big sea, including the Antarctic, world. Stumpy thinks so too. Fair dinkum.'

Interesting Words

Bellows:
a device that blows a current of air to make a fire burn more fiercely

Billabong:
waterhole

Billy:
tin container used to boil water

Bonzer:
excellent

Bunyip:
a creature in Aboriginal legends

Chook:
domestic chicken

Cooee:
a call used to attract attention in the bush. It rises in pitch on the last syllable—*ee*.

Cop this:
look at this

Dill:
a silly person

Dingo:
Australian wild dog, often brownish-yellow with pointy ears. It doesn't bark, but howls. Dingoes are known for attacking farm animals, such as sheep.

Dunny:	outside toilet
Fair dinkum:	true
Gammy:	injured
Hessian:	coarse, rough cloth made from jute, used for sacks or carpet backing
Honeybag:	native Australian beehive
Joey:	baby kangaroo
Meat safe:	a cabinet which keeps food cool
Quandong:	Australian native fruit
Spinifex:	spiky grass that grows in inland Australia
Swagman (or swaggie):	a bush traveller who carries a swag (a bundle of belongings) and earns money from odd jobs or gifts
Tank stand:	a framework to support a rainwater tank
Tucker:	food
What d'ya know:	Australian greeting, a way of saying hello

Look out for other titles in the **Audrey** series . . .

Audrey of the Outback

Meet Audrey Barlow—a girl with a lot on her mind. Her dad has gone away to work, her brother Price thinks he's too old for games, and little Dougie likes pretending to be a bird. But at least she's not alone. Audrey has a friend that is like no other, one who leads her to the hardest decision she has ever made.

Audrey Goes to Town

Audrey can't wait to get to the tiny town of Beltana. It's full of amazing things—like trains, glass windows and a shop that sells lollies. But when Mum gets sick, Audrey and her little brother Dougie must stay alone with Mrs Paterson. And Mrs Paterson is a strict old lady who looks like a burnt stick! Audrey soon starts to think that even a town full of people can't stop you feeling lonely.